CRYING CROCODILE

AN IRIS READ MYSTERY
BOOK 7

SUSAN CORY

The Crying Crocodile

© 2024

Published by Susan Cory

This book is a work of fiction. Names, characters, places and incidents either are products of the author's imagination or are used fictitiously. Any resemblance to actual events or locales or persons, living or dead, is entirely coincidental. All rights reserved. No part of this book may be used, including but not limited to, the training of or use by artificial intelligence, or reproduced in any manner whatsoever without written permission, except in the case of brief quotations embodied in critical articles and reviews or as permitted under the U.S. Copyright Act of 1976. No part of this publication may be reproduced, distributed or transmitted in any form or by any means, or stored in a database or retrieval system, without the prior written permission of the publisher.

ISBN- 979-8-9871784-7-8

CHAPTER 1

Out the Cessna's window, Iris Reid glimpsed a turquoise strip on the far horizon of the jungle. She nudged her boyfriend, Luc, who dozed in the seat next to her. "Look—the Pacific Ocean." The sea looked far more inviting than the frigid, gray waters off Massachusetts.

Luc rubbed a hand through his hair, making it stand up on end. He leaned over her to see out. A grin appeared. "We're really doing this."

"Thanks for talking me into it," Iris said. "Although I may feel differently once the surfing lessons begin, and I'm sunburned and covered in bruises."

"You'll do fine. We're here for fun, not competition."

Iris had her doubts. Luc was the owner and star chef of a popular Cambridge restaurant. He'd won a James Beard award and had graced the cover of Boston Magazine as "New England's sexiest chef." Iris's own architecture career was scaling new heights with her design of a museum in Harvard Square for a famous billionaire client. Neither one of them could exactly be described as laid-back.

"Kenneth, I think I see the resort. Are those thatched roofs by the beach? This place better not be rustic." The woman in the seat in front of Iris said the last word in a withering Southern drawl. The fortyish, heavily made-up blonde and her older partner had joined their plane in Dallas and transferred with them to the Guaria Morada Resort's private plane in Liberia, Costa Rica. Iris couldn't imagine the woman on a surfboard, but the resort billed itself as "luxury," so maybe she came for the pampering spa treatments, yoga, and gourmet dining.

"Don't worry, Margo. The owner assured me they have high-thread-count sheets and top-shelf hootch." Kenneth's tone was long-suffering. His long black hair was threaded with silver, and Iris bet he was the one who'd arranged the trip to tick off a sexy new sport on his list of accomplishments.

The hum of the single-engine plane changed register as it lowered in altitude. The dozen shades of green of the rainforest below came into focus. December was technically the dry season in Costa Rica, but the coast remained humid and lush year-round. The jungle extended all the way up to a ribbon of white sand edging the ocean.

"Tia, quick, give me the binocs," commanded an irritated male voice. Iris peeked through a gap to the seats behind them to see the speaker—a shaved-headed man in the process of lifting binocular straps from around a woman's neck.

Luc glanced back too, and softly groaned. He leaned over and whispered in Iris's ear, "He must have boarded before us. That's Eric Schwartz, a hot-shot L.A. chef. We got the same James Beard award last year, but his was for the West Coast. Total jerk."

So much for the two weeks not being a competition.

A young man met the plane at the landing strip. He introduced himself as Guillermo, one of the surfing instructors. He had the dark good looks of a Latin movie star and a boyish grin. An immaculate white van with **Guaria Morada Resort** emblazoned elegantly on the side was parked on the tarmac.

Iris could feel her hair lift away from her neck with frizz in the humid air. Guillermo distributed chilled towels and nearly frozen water bottles to the six passengers, then helped the pilot and co-pilot load suitcases into the back of the van. Margo and Kenneth climbed in the side door and parked themselves in the front row seats. This left Iris and Luc standing awkwardly beside Eric and his partner, a striking woman with locs pulled into a ponytail that trailed down her back.

"Hey, aren't you Luc Cormier?" the woman asked. "I'm Tia Moss." She nudged Eric. "You remember Luc from the James Beard dinner?" She turned to Iris. "Eric's a chef as well."

Eric gave Luc a bored look and a nod. "Hey, man. How's it going?"

Luc introduced Iris, and they all shook hands.

"Can you have this chat inside the van?" Margo called out, a bit too loudly. "The open door is letting out the air conditioning." She fanned herself with her plane ticket.

The four of them slipped into the remaining rows as Guillermo closed the van's rear hatch with a *click*. The drive to the resort took a brief ten-minutes through the thick jungle. Iris caught sight of some monkeys swinging through the canopy of trees. Monkeys! This place was so exotic.

As they entered a clearing, the main building of the resort appeared before them. It was a large three-story pavilion with a thatched roof and woven walls, set a hundred yards back from the turquoise waves breaking on the shore. The architectural style looked more Tahitian than Costa Rican to Iris's eyes, but she wasn't going to quibble. The effect was tropical. They piled out of the van and Iris could hear the chirping of birds and a howling of some unseen animals in the nearby underbrush.

Guillermo led them inside a pavilion with a soaring cathedral ceiling and exposed tree-trunk beams. A woman with cropped silver hair and a face like Audrey Hepburn awaited them. She had the effortlessly elegant posture of a ballerina. A tray of drinks sat on a table next to her.

"Welcome to the Guaria Morada Resort. My name is Sierra Winters. My husband and I created this resort, and we hope to provide you with a magical two weeks in our paradise." She gestured to an arrangement of upholstered chairs on one side of the large space. "Sit down and relax while Guillermo checks you in. We have Guaro Sours here, alcoholic and otherwise. It is the traditional drink of Costa Rica. Our porters will take you and your luggage to your casitas, where you can unwind before we meet back here at six for cocktail hour and orientation. My husband, Cal, will describe the surf program then, and I can fill you in on the yoga class schedule and other activities."

A young woman circulated with the tray of drinks as everyone found a seat. Iris was lifting the glass to her lips when she noticed a man enter the room. His short white hair stood up like a brush and his face was handsome and tan. He walked over to Sierra and kissed her on the lips. The man was slim and broad-shouldered like Luc and dressed in white linen. But the feature that caught Iris's gaze was the scar. It started at the right corner of his mouth and almost reached his ear.

The porter pocketed his tip with a slight bow and left Iris and Luc in their thatched-roof casita. It stood in the middle of eight others, spaced out along a stone path. The room was deceptively simple, with a canopied bed, white-washed walls, and mahogany louvers on the windows. A few pieces of artwork adorned the walls.

Iris approached an abstract painting hung over an antique desk and leaned closer to examine it. "I love that this resort has original art in the guest rooms."

Luc glanced up from unpacking his suitcase. "The magazine article said Cal and Sierra are showcasing Central American artists here. This place is a passion project for them."

"They've done a great job. I wonder who their architect was." Iris transferred shorts and shirts from her suitcase to a bureau drawer. "What's the deal with Eric Schwartz? Why don't you like him?"

Luc snorted. "I hate those competitive bro-types. At the James Beard dinner, he made some asinine comment while you were in the ladies room. I can't even remember what it was."

Iris was willing to bet that he remembered every word. She shook out several dresses and hung them in the large closet. As she turned back to the room, she saw Luc from the back, naked. He was stepping into his skimpy bathing suit. *Way to distract a girl.*

"We have an hour before cocktails. Ocean or pool?" he asked over his shoulder.

The infinity pool they'd passed on their way to the casita looked inviting. "Why not both?"

Luc sprawled on the bed, hands behind his head. "Greedy woman, get your suit on."

Ten minutes later, they headed to the pool. But Margo and Kenneth were already lounging on chaises there, two drinks in coconut shells on a table between them. Margo appeared to be dozing, her open mouth displaying her shiny white veneers. Kenneth was puffing on a cigar, studying his iPad. Iris swore to herself. She hated the smell of those stinkers, no matter how expensive the brand was.

Iris and Luc continued on toward the beach. It was deserted, and they quickly splashed into the ocean past the gentle break. The crystal-clear water was a perfect temperature, slightly cool, but warming up after a minute of thrashing around. The waves were about three feet tall, not too intimidating. She and Luc floated on their backs, rising and falling with the swells.

"This is heaven," Iris pronounced, eyes closed. When she got no response from Luc, she looked over. He was treading water, looking back at the beach with narrowed eyes, frowning. At Tia and Eric.

"Come on in," Iris shouted to the newcomers. "The water's great." She'd need to diffuse this tension between the two men before it ruined their vacation.

CHAPTER 2

Iris changed into a long, flowy dress for the cocktail hour. Twinkling lights lit the path from their casita to the main building. The buzzing of cicadas and clicking of tree frogs surrounded them. Iris was surprised that the sun set so early here, almost as early as back up North in Cambridge.

Luc held the door for her, and Iris entered the pavilion. Music with a Latin beat played softly through speakers. A few tables with bright tropical flowers and candles lined one side of the big open space. It looked like they were the last guests to arrive.

She and Luc threaded their way to the bar. The bartender's name tag read Sammy. He asked, "What can I get you?"

Iris knew that beer and cocktails were a more common choice in tropical countries, but she was in the mood for white wine. Maybe this fancy resort carried some varieties from Argentina or Uruguay.

At her request for wine, Sammy brightened. "Mrs. Duval brought us a case of her winery's Chardonnay and another case of their Petite Syrah. Their Napa vineyard is quite special. Would you like to taste the white first?"

He poured a small amount into a glass, and Iris sipped it. She held out the glass to Luc. "You need to try this. It's great. And no oakiness."

After Luc swished it around in his mouth and swallowed, his eyes got wide. He picked up the bottle on the counter and studied it. "I've never heard of the label before, but it's exceptional. I'd like to serve this in my restaurant. Who is Mrs. Duval? Is she here? I'd love to speak with her."

Sammy pointed her out on the far side of the room, then filled the rest of Iris's glass. "Over there, talking with Mr. Schwartz and Ms. Moss. She and her daughter drove across the country from San José. They arrived this evening to join the surf classes but sent the two cases of wine on ahead of them, so we had a chance to chill the white."

Iris looked over at the two women talking with Eric and Tia. They looked wholesome with make-up-free faces and wore short flowery sundresses under jean jackets. Both Kelly and her mother had strong features and dark eyebrows, but Kelly's build was larger and more athletic, like a field hockey player. Next to her, Lisa looked almost petite. There seemed to be a hint of steel behind their plain faces and clothes. After all, the two women ran an award-winning winery. Iris liked them on sight.

Tia raised the fashion quotient of the guests, wearing a long emerald-green column dress with tiny pleats. The silver bracelets on her arms stood out against her dark skin.

Luc asked to try the Syrah to see if the red was as impressive as the white. After taking several sips, he said to Iris, "We should go talk to her. Schwartz is probably putting in an order for his restaurant right now."

Iris rested a hand on his arm. "We're on vacation, remember? We'll be seeing the Duvals over the next two weeks. There'll be plenty of chances to talk."

"Right, right. Sorry." He turned to Sammy. "A Chardonnay for me as well please."

At that moment, Sierra and Cal walked up to the reception desk, which served as a focal point for the lounge, and turned to face the group. Conversation quieted down.

Sierra spoke first. "Welcome, cherished guests." She paused. "We built this resort five years ago and named it Guaria Morada after an endangered orchid, the national flower of Costa Rica. Our goal is to provide a bespoke experience for a limited group of guests over a two-week stay. We want to share our love of this country and its artists, both visual and culinary. Our chef, Santiago Vargas, uses the freshest local ingredients and turns them into his own creative vision."

Luc gave Iris an amused look.

"Most of you are here for the surfing program, which Cal will talk about in a minute. At breakfast each morning, I'll tell you about afternoon excursion options into the nearby villages or guided hikes through the rain forest to see waterfalls and birds. Surfing lessons will take place in the mornings. Video analysis of the morning's sessions will be screened directly after lunch for those who are interested. Later in the afternoon, I'll teach yoga classes on the Palm Court at four for those interested. Massages are offered anytime. You can find me to set it up. We have events scheduled for the evenings as well: live music and other surprises."

Eric shouted out, "Can we take any cooking classes?"

Sierra smiled. "Yes. I realize we have two renowned chefs as guests this session and you, along with anyone else, can join Chef Vargas in the kitchen for a cooking demonstration. We are here to tailor this vacation to your desires. You are equally welcome to just relax by the pool and enjoy our world-class meals." Sierra's eyes traveled to Margo. "Now I'll turn you over to Cal."

Cal wore a black dress shirt and black pants tonight. Coupled with his dramatic scar, he looked like a badass. Even his voice was gruff as he got right to the point. "The surfing classes will start in the mornings at nine when the waves are best suited for beginners. We'll meet out on the beach, and Guillermo and Mateo will be your instructors. We've made a schedule to fill the two weeks. You'll learn the basics in the first week, starting with ocean safety and wave etiquette. Tomorrow, you'll practice getting up on your boards while still high and dry on the beach. Then, you'll work up to that amazing thrill of balancing on your boards while riding the waves. Any questions?"

No one spoke up, so he continued. "By the second week, most of you will have reached the advanced beginner or even the intermediate level. We won't push you, but for those who feel steady enough, we'll teach you some more complicated moves. We want to leave you totally hooked on the sport after fourteen days. I have every expectation that all of you in the program will leave here as competent surfers."

Iris wasn't sure if she should be thrilled or terrified at the thought of being in this man's drill camp. What had she signed up for? She glanced at Luc. He looked excited. Maybe she could join Margo by the pool after making a good faith effort on the first day.

Cal continued. "Before we sit down to dinner, let me add one more thing. Our grounds here are like a Garden of Eden. Feel free to wander around during the day and ask any of us questions about the flora and fauna. But after the sun goes down, keep to the lighted pathways. Do not go wandering down to the beach or into the underbrush. This isn't Disneyland."

What kind of danger was Cal alluding to?

CHAPTER 3

Looking among the place cards set out on the tables, Iris discovered they were seated with Tia and Eric. Her effort to ease the strain between the two men had been somewhat successful, and she was starting to bond with Tia. The woman was a graphic designer in L.A. and had met Eric the previous year when she'd designed the menus for his restaurant, Twigs.

The four of them studied their menus in reverential silence for a few minutes.

"Heavily seafood based," Eric pronounced.

"With a Latin American spin on the spices," Luc added.

After they'd given their food and drink orders to the server, Iris asked Tia and Eric, "What do you think of this place?"

Eric leaned back in his chair. "I read about it in *Food & Wine* and knew what to expect. I'm here for the surfing, not the frills. I didn't grow up near the beach, so I'm stoked to commit two weeks of my time and come out a decent surfer."

"I have to admit, I'm a little intimidated by Cal," Tia said. "I wonder how involved he'll be in our lessons if those other two guys he mentioned will be teaching us."

"Hopefully, Cal's the hands-off organizer and we'll only interact with the kind, patient instructors," Iris said.

"I liked Cal's intensity," Luc said. "Didn't I read in that magazine article he was on the pro surfing circuit when he was younger?"

"Yeah, that's right," Eric said. "I hope we get a chance to watch him in action, although the waves here must be way below his level."

The server brought over the bottle of Duval Chardonnay they'd ordered and filled the four wine glasses. They clinked them in a toast. "Good times," Eric said.

"Do you serve this in your restaurant?" Luc asked him.

"No, Lisa Duval won't export it outside the Napa area except to a few places in San Francisco and to some private clients," Eric said. "This is the first time I've actually tasted it. It's not bad. Enjoy it while you're here."

"It's a shame. It's good stuff," Luc answered. "I'd like to talk with her. Find out how her family got into the business."

"You should ask her. It's an interesting story," Tia said.

Iris glanced over at the Duvals, who were sitting with Margo and Kenneth. A pairing of opposites. Yet they appeared to be having a lively conversation.

Their appetizers arrived, four different choices beautifully arranged on their plates. Iris's yellowfin tuna was garnished with cucumber and peanuts. Fried green tomato slices fanned along one side of Luc's grilled Mahi-Mahi. Eric had ordered the ceviche with a tomato granita and Tia had chosen a bright purple beet fritter with yogurt sauce drizzled across it.

"It certainly looks impressive," Eric said. "Now, for the taste test."

Appreciative noises followed for the next few minutes. Then, without asking, Eric slid some of Tia's fritter onto his fork and into his mouth. "Hmm. Charred something in that sauce. Maybe leek? Taste this, Luc. Is this charred leek with the basil?" He put a bite of it onto Luc's plate.

Luc looked at Tia apologetically.

She shrugged. "I'm used to it. Feel free."

Iris thought she would jab Eric's hand with her fork if he tried to eat off her plate. The men thoughtfully parsed Tia's fritter sauce, then went on to discuss the interesting granita accompanying Eric's ceviche. They finally agreed it was celery vinegar along with tomatoes and horseradish.

Tia got up and changed places with Eric so the men could converse more easily about every spice, herb, and trick technique in their meal. Once seated next to Iris, Tia asked her, "Have you met the Duvals yet?"

"Not yet. What are they like?"

"Very down-to-earth. Lisa, the mother, lost her husband in a horrible accident two years ago and took over the management of the vineyard. Her daughter, Kelly, got a B.S. in Enology from Oregon State. She's helping her mother try to expand the business, so they'll be able to export more of their wine."

"I'm sure Luc would like that," Iris said.

Tia put down her fork and dabbed the sides of her mouth with her napkin. "I read an article about the Duval family in *California Style & Culture* magazine. Lisa's in-laws have a well-respected vineyard in France, but her husband was determined to experiment with new techniques in America. He obviously succeeded. Their wine has a cult following among wine snobs."

"I guess Lisa and Kelly like to stay under the radar," Iris said, thinking of their low-maintenance look.

The main courses arrived and lived up to the impressive standards of the appetizers. Eric and Luc continued to discuss and critique the food and presentation. The women agreed it was nice to get a break from being on the receiving end of chef obsession.

After decaf espressos and spicy Chiliguaro shots, which tasted a little like Bloody Marys, Iris's eyelids felt heavy. It had been a long day.

She and Luc excused themselves, just as Eric was ordering more shots. They stopped by the two other tables, complimenting the Duvals on their wine, and wishing everyone good night. Once they'd left the pavilion and were on the path to their casita, Luc said, "Please tell me I'm not as obnoxious as Eric."

"Obsessed about food—yes. Obnoxious—no. I don't know how Tia puts up with him."

Luc took her arm, and Iris nestled into him, entwining her fingers with his. She gazed up at the moon. It would be full in a few days.

Maybe they could have a romantic dinner on their veranda that evening. She'd set it up as a surprise.

The reflection of the moonlight danced on the waves. As she watched, something on the beach caught her eye. The silhouette of a man with a rifle slung over his shoulder passing by quickly. She hissed, "Luc, look over there!"

But the man was gone.

CHAPTER 4

The next morning, as Iris lay beside Luc in bed, her perma-cold feet tucked between his calves, she convinced herself that the man on the beach must have been a security guard for the resort. Costa Rica was said to be the safest country in Central America, but this was a well-heeled crowd, and robberies would not be good publicity.

She could hear waves crashing nearby and see sunlight coming through the louvers, casting stripes against the far wall.

Luc nuzzled her neck. "Ready for your surfing debut, champ?"

"If I turn out to be lousy at this, will you think less of me?"

"Of course not. I'll just have to find someone else to go off and surf with." His crooked grin made it clear he was kidding.

It was strange that, as a brown-belt karate student, Iris felt self-conscious about undertaking a new sport, while Luc assumed he'd be good at it.

At nine o'clock sharp, she and Luc arrived at the beach. Iris regretted having eaten such a large breakfast from the laden buffet table. As she expected, all the guests except Margo were present. They wore bathing suits since the ocean was too warm to need wetsuits. Mateo, a dark bow-legged character who looked like he'd been shaving since birth, joined their instructor, Guillermo. The two men led the group out of the sun and over to a palapa, an open-sided hut woven from palm fronds. They all sat in the sand listening to Guillermo explain how to read the waves, surf safely, and follow surfing etiquette.

The instructors then matched each guest with a longboard three feet taller than their height, together with a leash to tether the boards to their leg. Mateo demonstrated how to wax the boards to provide traction against slipping.

Iris was surprised at how heavy and awkward the boards were to drag across the beach to the water's edge. Once there, Mateo instructed them on basic skills. He made it all sound easy: paddling out past the breaks, positioning yourself on the board, then popping up to a standing position. No sweat.

For the next half hour, they practiced their pop-ups on the shore, rising from their bellies onto one knee, then up to their feet. Iris had a little trouble folding her long legs under her, but soon got the hang of it. Kenneth needed the most help since his fat midriff was in his way. Mateo kept shouting, "Jump higher, Kenneth!"

When the four women and three men were somewhat competent with pop-ups, at least on dry land, the instructors spaced them out along the crescent of beach. Guillermo told them to paddle out past the breaks, turn around and try surfing back to shore. The three-foot-high waves suddenly looked much taller.

Iris wished she'd spent some time lifting weights to prepare for the paddling part. Lying face down on her board and trying to get out past the waves was exhausting. She noticed Luc had no trouble muscling through the crashing white water. He was strong from hefting heavy cartons of restaurant supplies and huge cast-iron pots.

After numerous tries, Iris finally got past the break. But by then, she barely had the strength to turn her board around and heft herself up on one knee. She immediately toppled over. The out-of-control board attached to her leg dragged her under the whitewash and water shot up her nose.

Was she having fun yet?

CHAPTER 5

At lunch in the pavilion, Luc couldn't stop talking about the rush he got when he first managed to stand upright on his board and ride a wave all the way to shore. The entire room was abuzz with excited surfing newbies recounting their awesome experiences.

Iris shoveled forkfuls of crab empanada into her mouth and chewed without tasting much.

Luc finally seemed to notice Iris's silence and looked sheepish. "Sorry, I've been going on and on. I checked you out a few times when we were in the water and saw you paddling. Did you get up on the board at all?"

She shook her head.

He frowned in concern. "Was it the pop-up that gave you trouble? Maybe we can practice this afternoon."

Iris's arms were so tired she'd barely been able to carry her plate back from the buffet table. "I need to rest. I'm sure I'll have better luck tomorrow," she said, with an assurance she didn't feel. She had assumed her weekly karate sessions would give her enough upper body strength for surfing, but apparently not. Now, her confidence wavered.

Slumping back in her chair, Iris caught sight of Tia two tables away. Eric was standing nearby, talking animatedly with Cal while Tia sat glumly eating. The women exchanged looks and Tia made a subtle thumbs-down. Iris gave her a tiny nod.

At least the food here lived up to expectations. Not that Iris had paid proper attention to her lunch. "How is your grouper?" she asked Luc.

"Wow—it's really fresh and grilled perfectly. But it's the mango and date salad that's blowing my mind. Do you want to taste it? There's coconut in the vinaigrette, but something else as well. I can't put my finger on it."

Iris glanced at his plate when a shadow fell over her. She looked up to find Sierra standing there.

"It's pureed palm hearts, the core of a bud of certain palm trees," Sierra explained.

"I thought it might be mashed artichoke hearts," Luc said.

"Yes, they taste similar. You must set up a time with Chef Vargas for a cooking demonstration."

"Eric and I are planning to do that after lunch."

"Good." She turned to Iris. "So, how was your first surfing class this morning?"

"I'm still trying to get the hang of it," Iris answered. "But Luc got in some good runs. I got so tired paddling, I didn't have the energy to stand up."

Sierra nodded. "That's very common, especially with women. Alas, our strength is mostly in our lower body. Why don't I set up an appointment for you with our masseuse this afternoon? Ana is amazing. She'll rejuvenate those tired muscles." Sierra took a small notebook out of her pocket and consulted it. "How about 2 o'clock?"

"Sure. Great idea."

"And both of you should come to my Yoga class at 4:00 to get in some good stretching."

After Sierra left, Iris and Luc ordered a pair of milky cortados for a caffeine boost. As their drinks arrived, Cal strode into the center of the space and the room quieted.

"Buenas tardes a todos, as we say in Costa Rica. Or good afternoon, everyone. I hope you all had a productive morning on the beach and in the waves. You may have noticed that I wasn't out there videotaping you on your first day. I figured I'd give you a grace period to get through the basics before you watched yourselves on the big screen. So, we don't have the usual after-lunch video analysis. Instead, for inspiration, I have a short film of Laird Hamilton, a true surf master, riding Oahu's Pipeline. These are monster waves, and he rides some of them for five, six minutes. If you keep surfing after our session here, who knows? You may someday find yourself searching for breaks like these."

Doubtful, Iris thought.

After the film, on her way back to their casita, Iris's phone chimed. It was a text from her friend, Ellie, back home in Cambridge. A photo showed her Basset hound, Sheba, with the dog's BFF, a Corgi named Merle. The two short-legged creatures were playing tug-of-war with a stuffed pig. Ellie had captioned it, "Sheba's play-date schedule is filling up."

Inside the casita's bedroom, Iris sat on the bed and texted back a heart emoji, relieved that her dog wasn't moping in her absence. She'd show the picture to Luc when he got back from talking to Chef Vargas, which might take a while.

Iris missed Sheba. She missed her routine in Cambridge. This was her first vacation in three years and the first one with Luc. *What is wrong with her?* Instead of huddling in a cold, sloppy New England winter, she was basking in a sunny paradise by the warm, blue ocean. The meals were a foodie's dream, she was with her gorgeous boyfriend, and was about to get a massage. Even if she never got up on the damn surfboard, she could have fun riding the waves on her stomach like a boogie board. Was her ego so fragile that she had to excel at everything?

Time to shed all pressure. And her attitude would improve if her arms didn't feel so sore. She found her cosmetic case on the bathroom counter and searched for the small bottle of muscle relaxants left over from who-knows-which past minor surgery. She washed down two pills with a swallow of water, then read the prescription label. Oops. She was only supposed to take one every four hours. At least she wouldn't be driving or operating heavy machinery.

It was almost time for her massage, so she stripped down to her underpants and wrapped herself in the resort's luxurious waffle-weave bathrobe. Sierra had given her directions to the massage hut on the far side of the resort, back behind the pavilion.

As she followed the curving paths, passing the other casitas, Iris noticed Lisa and Kelly Duval out on their veranda reading and waved to them. The grounds seemed otherwise deserted. People must be taking siestas during the heat of the day.

At the end of the path bordering the jungle, she found the round thatched hut Sierra had described. It had a row of square openings high-up in the curved walls, a way to let out warm air and to cool the interior naturally. As she approached, a pair of tittering monkeys jumped up onto the roof and swung over to the trees.

Iris tapped on the door and a smiling young woman with a long black braid gestured her in.

"*Hola*. Welcome. I am Ana. And you are Ms. Reid, yes?"

"Call me Iris," she said.

"Tell me what parts of your body you would like me to focus on today."

Iris was relieved that Ana's English was good, if distinctly accented. Her own Spanish was sketchy, at best.

"My shoulder blades and arms, mainly."

"Ah, first time surfing?" Ana asked.

"Yes, and the paddling wore me out."

"I see much sore shoulders here. I will fix you up."

Ana held up a sheet as Iris hung up her robe and scooted onto the massage table. Some quiet music, which sounded like water trickling in a fountain, played in the background. Iris rested her forehead on the headrest. The masseuse rubbed oil on her shoulders and Iris inhaled the soothing scent of jasmine. Ana's deft hands worked steadily, lulling her into a happy stupor. She soon felt so-o-o relaxed, indifferent to time.

Sometime later, Iris was startled awake by the sound of angry voices. Were two men arguing in Spanish? Where were they? She lifted her head and looked around. Ana was industriously massaging her left leg, humming, and ignoring the minor commotion.

The masseuse smiled at her. "Is the pressure okay?

"It's good, thanks." Iris put her head back down, but listened intently. The sound was coming from outside the hut, through the high openings in the wall. She tried to understand what they were saying and caught the words: "Pero ellos nos pertenecen." A second man with a deep, resonant voice responded, "Julio, no! Es demasiado peligroso." Then the conversation stopped abruptly.

Iris needed to look up those words in the Spanish translation app on her phone as soon as she got back to the casita. "Peligroso" sounded like trouble.

CHAPTER 6

On her walk back to the casita, Iris's body felt like jelly and her mind like cotton. She focused on getting her legs to move forward as steadily as possible along the path. When she reached the pool area, she spotted Kenneth and Margo stretched out in the same lounge chairs as before. Iris dreaded making conversation with them, but the pills she'd taken earlier had kicked in big time and she needed to sit down. When she eased herself gingerly onto a chair, their eyebrows raised with concern.

"You feeling all right, hon?" Margo asked, sliding her sunglasses up on top of her head and squinting at her.

"Just a little woozy. I need to rest a minute."

"Too many mojitos?" Kenneth nodded. "Know the feeling."

Iris took some deep breaths. A young man folding towels in the pool hut watched her, concern in his eyes. He reached under the counter, then approached her with a frosty bottle of water held out. She noticed a brightly colored Scarlet Macaw tattooed on his right biceps. He looked to be about twenty years old and had warm liquid brown eyes.

"Are you all right?" he asked in heavily accented English.

"Yes." Iris took the bottle. "Gracias."

"De nada," he responded, before turning back to the hut.

Margo's eyes followed the retreating man, and she leaned closer to Iris. "That's Julio, the pool boy. Nice, huh?"

Wait, *Julio*? Was he the same man she'd overheard by the massage hut? It must be a fairly common name.

She took a big gulp of water, then whispered to Margo, "Did Julio just come on duty?"

Margo's eyes got wide, and she cackled. "You want to know his schedule? You cougar! With that blond hottie boyfriend, you're still checking out the local talent? You do have good taste, though. That god-bod—mmm."

Kenneth peered over his sunglasses at Iris and winked. "We all have our appetites. Especially here in the tropics, right?"

Ugh. "No, I was wondering if anyone was around earlier…oh, never mind. I feel better now." She got up and headed toward the pool hut, feeling two sets of eyes salaciously drilling into her back. She wanted to hear Julio speak more in order to compare voices.

"Julio, do you know where and when the yoga class meets?"

"Sí. Señora Winters teaches near the coconut grove over there at four o'clock." He gestured to a clearing to the left of the beach.

It was the same voice, the same Julio.

When Iris reached their casita, she found Luc on the veranda resting in the hammock.

"How was your massage? You look—wait. Are you drunk?"

"No-o-o. The massage just loosened me up. My arms feel much better." She swung them around to demonstrate. "You should get one."

Luc looked at her skeptically. "Do you still want to go to the yoga thing? You might need a nap."

"Uh-uh. I'm totally up for yoga. You?"

"Yeah, I need it. Spending so much time in the kitchen hunched over the stove has messed up my back."

Iris glanced at her watch. "We'd better get ready. Oh, by the way, do you know what peligroso means in Spanish?"

Luc tipped his head. "I know that pericoloso means dangerous in

Italian. They could be the same. Where did you hear that word? I hope no one was talking about danger around here."

Luc would be annoyed if Iris manufactured a mystery where there was none. She needed to stop seeing intrigue everywhere she went. This was their vacation. Even if there *was* something fishy going on at the resort with the staff, it was none of her business.

CHAPTER 7

After yoga class, Sierra invited Iris and Luc to join her and Cal that night at their table. Iris looked forward to learning more about the resort's founders over dinner.

At cocktail hour, with the tropical sun headed fast for the horizon, Iris paused outside the pavilion to admire two huge clay pots flanking the main door. They were glazed a distinctive celadon color.

"Wouldn't a set of pots like this look great outside your restaurant?" She asked Luc. "I wonder if they're made around here."

"The resort features local art, so I'll bet they were." Luc studied them. "Would you need to put something in them, like branches?"

"You could do that and string them with little twinkling lights."

"Maybe we can visit the potter's studio and see what they have," Luc said. "Let's talk to Sierra about it."

They entered the pavilion to the sound of reggae music coming through the speakers. The pulse of the music was compelling, but thankfully the sound was soft enough to allow conversation.

"What can I get you?" Luc asked. "White wine, a Guaro Sour?"

Iris's brain haze from the pills she'd taken earlier had finally dispersed. The sight of Margo wiggling her hips over by Kenneth gave her a sudden inspiration. "How about a mojito?"

"Yes, ma'am." Luc headed to the bar.

Iris didn't notice Tia's approach until she heard her throaty voice close by. "Why does every rich older guy with a trophy girlfriend wear a David Yurman bracelet and Tod's driving shoes to appear young and cool? I'm surprised he doesn't have an earring."

Iris made a catlike clawing motion at Tia and glanced over to verify Kenneth's accessories. "Where's your obsessive chef? Did Eric have a good time interrogating Chef Vargas?"

Tia pointed with her chin. "Over at the bar with *your* obsessive guy. I hope the poor chef didn't have to disclose all his secret recipes."

"Those two will be separated tonight because we're sitting with Sierra and Cal."

"Well, la de da. I hope our fearless leaders are prepared to discuss every herb in every sauce with Luc."

This evening, Tia wore a yellow halter neck maxi dress with a medallion pattern. "Where do you get such great clothes?" Iris asked. "You're almost as cool as Kenneth."

"Ooh, sick burn. There's a gem of a vintage shop on La Brea Ave."

Eric and Luc returned from the bar, handing each of the women their drinks.

Iris delicately tasted her mojito as Luc watched.

"It has a little coconut in it," he said. "Do you like it?"

"Mmm. Tasty." She took a good long sip, starting to relax into vacation mode. The music was as intoxicating as her drink.

Eric's voice rose above the deep Jamaican backbeat. "So, what do you do, Iris?"

She looked over at him. "I'm an architect."

He shoveled some sea salt potato chips into his mouth. "Hmph. I took a drafting class in high school. Don't you find it boring?"

Tia elbowed him in the side. "Eric! That's rude!"

Iris thought of possible responses, then decided not to bother. *Luc is right. Eric is a douche.*

"Oh, sorry.' Eric laughed too loud. "I'm trying to be curious about other people's lives."

"Iris is designing a museum now." Luc said. "Roku made a film about her creative process."

Eric's face remained unimpressed.

"That's way cool," Tia said. "Is the film out now? I want to see it."

Iris was relieved when Sierra and Cal joined their group and shifted the focus away from her.

"Is everyone enjoying their first day?" Sierra asked.

The group made small talk until it was time for Iris and Luc to peel off with Cal and Sierra toward their dinner table. They sat down and ordered a fresh round of drinks. Iris switched to club soda to pace herself.

"How was your massage?" Sierra asked Iris.

"Fantastic. Ana really knows how to work out the kinks."

"We're lucky to have her. We met Ana and her cousin Julio years ago, living in an orphanage that we now support in Santa Elena. The kids there are offered a variety of trades to study, and we try to find jobs for them when they graduate."

So, Julio and Ana are cousins. Ana would have recognized his voice.

"You're both making an incredible impact here," Luc said. "Between showcasing Costa Rican art, supporting the orphanage, and providing employment, it must be satisfying to know that you're giving back to the community."

Cal beamed. "Sierra and I fell in love with this country when we came here on vacation ten years ago. The Ticos, as Costa Ricans call themselves, are so good-hearted. They refer to their way of life as 'pura vida' which translates as 'pure life,' but embraces so much more about sustainable living, and on so many levels."

Sierra reached for Cal's hand. "We were living in Sausalito. Cal was teaching surfing, and I was a Yoga instructor. The long, foggy winters got to us, and we wanted a simpler lifestyle. Once we came here, we were hooked."

"I can understand why," Iris said. "It's a beautiful country."

At that moment, the server delivered their drinks and took dinner orders. Luc asked a few detailed questions about how tonight's Cubera snapper was prepared before committing to it.

There was a lull in the conversation, and Iris felt obliged to fill it. "I noticed the giant clay pots outside the pavilion. Is the potter from around here? We would love to visit the studio and hopefully buy some pieces for Luc's restaurant."

Sierra seemed to consider this. "It's a small place, but I think we can arrange that. The potter's name is Violetta, and she's the sister of Mateo, your surfing instructor."

Luc laughed. "Everyone around here seems to be related."

"I know," Cal grinned. His laugh lines collided with the scar running down his cheek, giving him a malevolent look. "We know a lot of siblings with no parents from our work with the orphanage. We try to find them work here or patronize their businesses."

Sierra pointed at Cal with an index finger. "Isn't Mateo going into the village tomorrow to run some errands? Maybe he can drive Iris and Luc there to see his sister's studio."

Cal nodded. "And there's a small museum in Santa Elena worth visiting, if you like pre-Columbian artifacts."

"That would be great." Iris noticed a quick frown pass across Sierra's face. Maybe she worried that their big-city expectations would be too high for a small, local museum. "I took an art history course in college about that era, but it mainly focused on Mexican traditions. I'd love to see a few examples from this area."

Their appetizers arrived and conversation quickly became food focused.

Iris didn't realize until she and Luc were back in the casita that she'd forgotten to ask the Winters about the armed guard she'd seen on the beach the night before. No big deal. She was pretty sure her hosts were just safeguarding the resort., and of course its guests.

CHAPTER 8

Early the next morning, a strange sound shook Iris awake. Lying in the semi-darkness, she heard scampering footsteps on the roof of the casita, followed by a loud, whooping roar. The noise resonated in her bones. The sheets next to her rustled as Luc sat up in bed. "What the hell was that?"

"Monkeys, I'll bet. They're called howler monkeys for a reason." Iris reached for her phone on the bedside table. "Six a.m." she announced.

"It's barely dawn." Luc swung his legs out of bed. "I'm going to have a word with those chuckleheads." He picked up a mango from the fruit basket on the desk and stalked out to the veranda.

Iris ran after him, holding out a bathrobe. "Be careful. They might bite."

He wrapped the bathrobe around his naked torso. "I may bite back."

"And don't hurt them!"

The sky had lightened enough that Iris and Luc could see two long-haired black monkeys, each the size of Sheba, sitting placidly on the roof. They looked unperturbed by their glaring audience until Luc pitched the mango near the one not eating leaves, presumably the noisemaker. Both animals scurried off before the mango connected. They jumped onto the adjacent casita's roof, then shimmied down to the ground, disappearing into the dense jungle.

Iris followed Luc back to bed. "Well, that got my adrenaline pumping. I'm wide awake now."

Luc undid his sash and let his bathrobe fall to the floor. "Hmm. I wonder how we can tire ourselves out so we can fall asleep again?"

At breakfast in the pavilion, everyone was buzzing with complaints about the monkeys waking them up so early.

While the crowd filled their plates at the generous buffet table, Eric spoke up loudly. "We have Luc to thank for pitching something at the monkeys to chase them away. We saw you out our window. Bravo, dude."

Luc took a small bow. Iris glanced around for Sierra and Cal, afraid that they might not approve of his intervention. But Sierra just sighed as she spooned honey into her tea on the other side of the buffet table. "I apologize for those damn howler monkeys. They're literally the loudest land mammal on the planet. They send out howls at dawn and dusk as a warning to other clans to stay off their turf. I guess they picked this morning to pay us a visit. I'll get some of the staff to chase them away tonight if they're still around."

"It probably wouldn't be so bad if they weren't right up on the casita roofs," Luc said.

Sierra sat down at Iris and Luc's table. "I know. The males have a special bone in their throats to give extra resonance to their calls."

Iris's architectural instincts sprang to attention. "In New England, we have sharp metal guards on our roofs to break up the snow and ice in winter. I wonder if something like that could be attached to the roofs here to keep the monkeys off."

"Interesting idea," Sierra said. "How would it look?"

Iris cradled her second cortado and considered. "You could set pieces of sharpened bamboo along a track and mount it to the thatch. The prongs wouldn't have to be long, and the color could blend in. It would be easy to construct. I can work up a sketch for you later, after our surfing lesson."

"That would be great," Sierra said. "But I hate to put you to work while you're on vacation."

Iris waved her hand. "It's no big deal. I sketch all the time, anyway. If it keeps the monkeys off the roofs, it will be worth the effort."

CHAPTER 9

After breakfast, Iris and Luc headed for the beach. Iris was determined to take it easier with the paddling today and allow herself some rest periods, but she was equally determined to get up on her board.

Eric called out to them, his arm rising over his shining, shaved head in an enthusiastic wave. "Hey, Luc. Let's see who can stand up the longest today."

"You're on," Luc yelled back.

Tia, dressed impractically for surfing in a yellow bikini, approached Iris with a rueful grin. "I'll be happy to get up on my feet at all."

"Same."

The Duvals and Kenneth arrived together, and the whole group moved over to the palapa to be matched up with their assigned gear. Once they had all dragged or carried the heavy longboards across the beach, Guillermo and Mateo tossed them each a disk of wax the size of a hockey puck and reminded them how to apply it.

Iris rolled up her phone in a towel and set it on the sand back from the water. She told Luc, "I'm going to try to get a picture of you catching a wave."

"Maybe you should wait until the end of the session when I get better at this." He smoothed his long hair back, securing it with an elastic band. "How about you? You want me to get a shot of you standing up triumphantly today?"

"That's a *big* if," she answered as she industriously rubbed wax onto the deck of her surfboard.

After a few minutes, the instructors spaced the students out along the beach so they wouldn't run into each other. Eric positioned himself next to Luc. Mateo then led them through a series of stretches. After they'd attached their Velcro leashes to their ankles, they turned to face the water.

Iris sent up a silent prayer to the surf gods, whoever they were, before pushing her board into the shallow froth. After a few strokes while kneeling, the stiffness in her arms began to disappear. Once the water was deep enough, she slid onto her stomach and paddled deeply through the whitewash with the rest of the lineup. By timing her movement between the oncoming waves, she was able to push her board out beyond the break and was soon bobbing around in the calmer deep water. First mission accomplished.

Pivoting the board to face back toward the beach didn't require much exertion. She looked around to see that the three men and Kelly were also out there with her beyond the break. Luc looked over and gave her a thumbs up.

Iris peered over her shoulder to access the oncoming breakers. She lay there, gathering her energy and courage. After a few moments, she began to paddle wildly, trying to get ahead of a promising wave. But she had timed it wrong, and it passed under her, lifting her, then leaving her behind. She caught sight of Luc hopping gracefully to his feet and riding the same wave in to shore. *That* was how it was supposed to look.

Iris watched several more waves pass, calculating when she'd need to start paddling. And this time she managed to catch the break before the crest, got up on one knee, and then froze. She rode that way for several surprised seconds, then tumbled over. Nevertheless, those few unstable seconds at the peak made her pulse race. She'd caught a wave and almost stood up! She spent the next hour repeating the sequence until she actually stood upright and rode the wave all the way to the shore. As she crashed through the whitewater foaming along the beach, she looked up to see Luc sitting in the sand, holding her phone up to his eye.

"Did you film me?" Iris asked, dragging her board onto the sand. "Did I look awesome?"

"Like a surf goddess!" he assured her, handing over the phone.

She leaned over and replayed the video, then made a face. "I see room for improvement."

"That's why it's lucky we're here for two whole weeks." Luc stood, tucking his board under an arm, and splashed back into the water.

After two hours, Iris decided to call it a day, or a morning at least, with time to rest before lunch. She signaled to Luc by pointing toward the casitas, and he nodded.

Back in her room, Iris showered and changed. Her sketchbook lay on the desk. She scooped it up along with a Razor point pen and headed out to the veranda. Squinting her eyes, she visualized the size of the monkeys from that morning. It took less than thirty minutes and one rickety climb on top of a chair to examine the roof construction to produce a sketch of an anti-monkey roof barrier.

CHAPTER 10

Iris found Sierra in the pavilion at lunchtime and showed her the sketch. She explained what materials to use and how the strips should attach to the casita roofs.

"This is wonderful," Sierra said. "Thank you. I hope this didn't take time away from your surfing lesson."

Iris assured her it was no problem.

"Oh, and Mateo said he can take you and Luc into Santa Elena this afternoon to see his sister's pottery studio."

"Are you sure he doesn't mind?" Iris asked.

"Not at all. He's going anyway. He asked if you would meet him in the parking lot at one o'clock."

"Great. I'll tell Luc."

An hour later, Iris and Luc found Mateo waiting for them in his beat-up Hyundai. "I hope you don't mind. My car is not up to resort standards."

"Neither is my van at home," Luc assured Mateo as he got into the front seat and Iris slid into the back, next to a bulging laundry bag.

"You are so kind to let us tag along on your visit home," Iris said. "I can't wait to see your sister's other pieces. Do you know if she ships to the States?"

"I think so. You can ask her." Mateo shifted the car into gear and backed out. "It will take us about a half hour to get there." He turned on the radio. Loud Spanish hip-hop blasted from the speakers. If the air-conditioning in the car worked at all, it was not turned on, but at least the windows were half-open, letting in a breeze.

They bumped along the rutted road until brightly colored stucco houses with tile roofs came into view. The houses became denser, interspersed with shops. Soon they arrived at a town square with an open green plaza in the center. Mateo parked. "Here we are—this is Santa Elena. I'll take you to Violetta's studio and introduce you. You can visit with her, then walk around if you like. There's an ice-cream shop and a few other stores in the square. I'll be done with my laundry and errands at about three and we can meet back at the car, okay?"

Mateo led them down a sloping ramp alongside a four-story apartment building to a basement door around the back. When he knocked, a young woman answered. Her luxurious black hair was waist-length, and she wore a white cotton tunic and pants. She smiled shyly, ushering them in. Pointing to herself, she said, "I, Violetta. My English is not so good." She turned to Mateo and said something quickly in Spanish. He shrugged and answered, also in Spanish, then retreated to the door.

"I'll leave you now," Mateo said. "See you at the car at three."

The studio was small, with white-washed walls and a concrete floor. Half a dozen finished pots and vases stood up against the back wall. Iris moved closer to examine them. They were glazed in the same beautiful shade of greyish green as the pots she had seen.

Violetta gestured toward the two largest ones, still smaller than the ones at the resort. "These are already sold, but the others are for sale."

Shelves holding cups and bowls lined a side wall. Iris was surprised by how few pieces she saw, about two dozen in all.

"Do you ever make more of the big size pots like the ones at the resort?" Iris asked.

"Oh, those were very difficult. They barely fit in kiln. Several broke before those two are okay." Violetta gestured toward an enormous brick bee-hive-shaped structure in a corner of the room. A potter's wheel and large sink stood next to it.

Luc walked over to study the bowls. "These are nice." He held one up to show Iris.

She walked over to see them better. "Do you ship pieces to the United States? We're interested in buying two big pots, like the ones at the resort."

Violetta looked alarmed. "Big like that? Oh, no. Too fragile to ship. I could make smaller ones, maybe." She held her hand above the floor to indicate two feet in height.

Iris looked at Luc. "That scale wouldn't be big enough for outside the restaurant door, but one might be nice in the entryway to our loft."

They discussed pricing. Violetta named a high figure, well beyond what they had in mind. So instead, Iris and Luc chose four different colored bowls from the shelf, figuring that these could fit in their suitcases, and would make nice souvenirs from the trip. Iris paid with four green 10,000 Costa Rican Colon bills, grateful that she had changed dollars into some local currency back at the airport in San José.

Violetta wrapped the bowls carefully in paper and handed Iris a bag with a smile. "Gracias."

It was only 2:00 when Iris and Luc returned to the street, and the sun was hot overhead.

"What should we do now?" Luc asked. "There's the ice cream shop over there."

"I'm still full from lunch. Let's walk around the plaza and look in the shops."

They passed a T-shirt shop selling cheap souvenirs. Iris bought a few postcards. She had the sense that Santa Elena wasn't a big tourist town. The rest of the stores seemed to be geared to the locals.

"What's that building over there?" Luc pointed to a two-story Spanish Colonial building with a curved cornice on top. As they approached, they saw a brass plaque next to the door reading Museo de Santa Elena.

"That's the museum Cal mentioned. I bet it will be cool inside." Iris climbed several steps to a thick wood door and tried the heavy cast-iron handle. It opened. The dimly lit interior felt twenty degrees cooler. A tiny older woman dressed in black sat behind a desk reading by the light of a table lamp. She looked up from her book. "Bienvenido."

"Hola. ¿Hablas inglés?" Iris said hopefully. She hated not being able to speak the native language. "Are you open?"

"I speak a little. Yes, we are open." The woman said.

Luc fitted a 5,000 Colon bill through the slot in a metal box next to an entry fee sign.

"Leave bag please and go there." The woman pointed to a door to her left.

Iris left her purse and the bowls. When they headed into a room containing several glass-fronted cases, lights snapped on, illuminating the displays inside.

"It looks like it's mainly pottery." Iris tried to read the sign on a side wall. She could only interpret the date, 500 BCE. "Really old pottery."

Luc squatted down to examine a two-foot-high jar with a monkey perched on top. "I think this one is made from jade. Look at the workmanship on it."

Iris thought back to her undergraduate art history class on Pre-Columbian artifacts. "I bet you're right. It looks like an incense burner. Mayan and Olmec cultures often used jade."

As they progressed through the displays, they found several more artifacts with animals on top, mixed in with old coins and ceramic ceremonial pieces. There were three rooms that looped around the entrance space. When they got to the last room, they noticed a single glass case, spot lit from several angles. Inside was a jade urn, much larger and more ornate than the others. On top of it sat a crocodile. A pattern of tiny, raised dots covered the jar, and the animal was intricately detailed. Under its right eye sat an enormous green stone.

"Holy moly. Is that an emerald?" Luc asked.

Iris moved closer and squatted to see better. "Do you think so? It's the size of something Elizabeth Taylor would wear around her neck. Shouldn't this be in the big museum in San José?" She tried to read the plaque set into the display stand. There were several sentences in Spanish that she couldn't decipher. The heading read El Cocodrilo Llorando 500 BCE. "I wonder what Llorando means." She took half a dozen pictures on her phone, then poked her head out into the vestibule and cleared her throat.

The museum attendant looked up from her reading.

"The crocodile urn—is that a real emerald?"

The woman followed Iris back into the third gallery. She regarded the museum's star exhibit and smiled proudly. "Yes, real emerald! Very big."

"And what does Llorando mean?" Luc asked.

The attendant reached a fist up to her eye and made whimpering noises, mimicking crying.

"Crying? The crying crocodile?"

"Si. Crying Crocodile. A tear."

Then the woman shook her head sadly. "The crying crocodile of Santa Elena is only one left. The others stolen. Thief not found."

Iris wasn't sure what others the woman was alluding to. She knew that antiquity looting was a problem in general, especially in the early twentieth century, when many countries didn't have the budget to protect their cultural heritage. The only thing she could think to say was, "that's terrible. Lo lamento." She wasn't sure if that was the right expression.

The three of them moved back to the entryway. Realizing the time, Iris and Luc excused themselves and left the museum to find Mateo outside. He was leaning against his car, looking at his phone. He saw them and waved. "Did you find any pottery you liked?"

Iris held up her bag. "We bought some bowls, but Violetta didn't have many pieces for sale right now."

Mateo unlocked the car. "I think she sold some pieces recently. Sorry about that."

"No, it was fun to see her studio and I love the bowls we did buy." Iris slid gingerly into the sweltering back seat, quickly cranking both windows open.

"And we found a great little museum afterward," Luc added.

Mateo turned his key in the ignition. "Yeah, it's tiny, but has some good things."

"I love that Crying Crocodile statue." Luc said. "It must be the pride of the town."

Mateo pulled out of the parking space. "Yeah, it's pretty cool."

CHAPTER 11

When Iris and Luc were back at their casita, Luc brought his laptop to the veranda and set it on the table. He looked up Thefts of Artifacts in Costa Rica. A story from the previous week in the Tico Times, Costa Rica's leading English-language newspaper, came up in the browser. Iris sat next to him on the loveseat and read the article along with him.

Valuable Artifact Stolen from Garza

On Christmas evening, a pre-Hispanic jeweled incense burner known as The Hunting Eagle, from around 500 BCE, was stolen from the Museo de Garza. The thieves bypassed the security system, and the Hunting Eagle was the only artifact they took. The theft wasn't discovered until the museum's head docent, Muriel Gomes, arrived shortly before 9 am on December 26 to open the building. "It was a treasured piece of our history," Ms. Gomes stated.

This was the third artifact stolen this month from a quartet of incense burners incorporating an animal and a valuable jewel, each housed in a separate village. In similar robberies on December 18 and 21, the Leaping Jaguar of Maquenco, with its magnificent sapphire, and the Dancing Serpent of Mafambu with a large ruby embedded in its tail, were stolen from their display cases in Maquenco's Town Hall and Mafambu's Museo.

The renowned Tica Archaeologist Ramón Santos discovered the cache of buried artifacts in 1991 when he was excavating the Dolce Nombre site for relics from around 500 BCE. The Mayans were not thought to have lived as far south as Costa Rica, but other indigenous peoples did inhabit the area. These tribes were influenced by cultures from what is now Colombia and they displayed sophisticated engineering skills which can be seen at the Guayabo ruins.

Instead of handing his finds over to the Museo Nacional de Costa Rica, Ramón Santos chose to divide the antiquities, including the quartet of jeweled incense burners, among the nearest four villages to the archeological site to allow the locals closer access to their priceless cultural heritage.

A piece of lapis lazuli, clutched in The Hunting Eagle's talons, was the least valuable of the quartet's stones, compared to the emerald, sapphire and ruby embedded in the other three. But the authorities speculate that the highly selective mastermind behind these robberies might want to add the set to a personal collection with no intention of selling the stones separately on the black market.

The Crying Crocodile of Santa Elena is still safe in its village museum for the time being, and security measures have been stepped up. The authorities are actively searching for the thieves.

Anyone with information about these two robberies is urged to contact the hotline anonymously at: 800/2376-9667.

Luc sat back in his chair and whistled. "This sounds like a big deal. Why didn't Mateo mention it? Maybe he isn't in touch with the villages' concerns now that he works at the resort."

"I'll bet that archeologist is kicking himself for not donating them to the museum in San José," Iris said. "Still, it was a nice thought, giving these treasures to the locals so they can admire them."

"And easily steal them," Luc said. "The thief now has three urns. I wonder how long before the fourth one disappears?"

"The security at the Santa Elena Museum didn't look very state-of-the-art," Iris said. "Hopefully, there were invisible sensors tied in to the police station."

"Doubtful."

"I've heard about trafficking in antiquities but didn't know it was a problem here. Costa Rica always seems like such a safe country."

"Criminals operate everywhere," Luc replied. "It might even be easier for them to steal things in a country that isn't accustomed to a lot of serious crime."

"The article speculated that the mastermind might be assembling these relics for a private collection," Iris said.

Luc laughed. "Sounds like something out of a James Bond movie. A villain sitting in a secret room, admiring his stash of stolen art over a crystal glass of rare brandy."

CHAPTER 12

When Iris awoke the next morning, her first thought was that it was New Year's Eve. But celebrating it in the tropics felt strange. New Year's Eves were bitterly cold in Boston. *Wicked* cold. She'd always plan to go to First Night events in Boston and to check out the ice sculptures, only to chicken out when the thermometer plunged below freezing. And for the last few years, Luc was always tied up cooking at night. She glanced over at him still asleep. At least they'd be together this year.

Sierra had told the guests there would be a special New Year's Eve dinner on the beach that night. And on Thursday, there would be a hike to a waterfall offered. Iris wasn't used to group activities. She wasn't sure she liked the prospect, considering how annoying certain members of the group were.

After breakfast, Iris and Luc walked down to the beach to find Mateo and Guillermo staring out at the ocean, muttering to each other. The waves looked bigger than yesterday's.

Tia was already there. She sidled over to Iris and tipped her head toward the instructors. "Tell me, do our fearless leaders look nervous to you? There aren't any sharks around here, are there?"

Iris looked over. As she did, the instructors turned to face the two women with their perfect professional smiles intact.

"Are we ready to surf?" Guillermo asked, a bit too enthusiastically.

By the time Iris pushed her board into the whitewater, she noted that the waves were much bigger today. She struggled to push through the break and then found it a challenge to pivot her board around to face the beach. When an intimidating wave rose behind her, she moved into position. But at the last minute she lost her nerve and stayed belly-down, riding the back of the big wave. *What is with this surf today?*

Iris fought her way through the churning water onto the shore and decided to stay there for now. Maybe she would video Luc. He could probably handle these waves. Out of the corner of her eye, she noticed Cal jogging up the path, beckoning Guillermo and Mateo over to the palapa. Isolated words drifted over. "Rogue … from Mexico … signal in." Cal held up a pair of binoculars and looked out to sea.

Was something dangerous happening, maybe a strong riptide forming or a serious storm?

Luc was turning his board around. Eric was with him out beyond the break, bobbing in the choppy water. Kelly had caught a wave that looked taller than the earlier ones. She barely managed to keep her balance, but successfully reached the beach.

Mateo blew a series of short, piercing shrieks on his whistle while Cal and Guillermo frantically ushered Kenneth, Lisa, and Tia out of the shallow water, shoving their boards back onto the sand.

Iris stood up and waved her arms at Luc. Had he noticed the ocean starting to rear up much further out? It looked like Eric was shouting to Luc, who then turned his head toward the waves growing behind them.

Eric took off on the next breaker, remaining on his stomach. As it reached its peak, the wave seemed to hesitate, holding his board in thrall, before crashing straight down with great force. A few seconds later, Eric's head reappeared in the froth, the end of his board popping up a beat later. He scrambled for his footing on the sandy bottom. Tia and Mateo hurried into the shallow water to help him stagger to shore.

Cal jogged into the ocean with a surfboard under his arm. He spoke briefly with Eric, continued running, then slid onto his board. Immediately after another large wave broke, he paddled furiously to reach beyond the break where Luc was waiting, nervously looking back at the oncoming waves. Cal paddled over to him, and they lay on their boards, conferring side-by-side, rising and falling with each increasing swell.

From the beach, everyone's eyes were glued to the waves as they grew taller and taller. Lisa covered her mouth in alarm. By now, the peaks seemed to be six feet high, as tall as Luc. Tia wrapped a towel around Iris's shoulders, and Iris realized she was shaking. Guillermo reassured her. "Cal's got this. He's surfed in twenty-foot waves."

"But Luc hasn't," Iris snapped.

Cal pointed out to sea, and it looked like the two men were about to make a move. Iris saw a wave rise under them as they paddled to get ahead of the next one. As the second wave rose, Iris gasped at its expanding size. Cal immediately hopped to his feet, arms spread, stance low on his board. Ten feet over, Luc remained prone, but paddling furiously. They caught the crest together and started the steep descent. Suddenly, Luc's board shot up in the air. His body travelled in the opposite direction. One of Luc's arms windmilled while the other one, caught in his leash, slammed into the rocketing board. He disappeared into the churning whitewater.

Iris ran into the surf. She scanned for some sign of Luc in the agitated water. A powerful undertow kept pulling her out to sea, but she kept her footing.

Cal was nearby. He undid his foot leash, slid his board over toward Mateo to take ashore, then swam back out with Iris. Cal reached the spot first and dove into the froth. A moment later, he resurfaced, holding an unconscious Luc, Cal's arm across his chest. By now, Guillermo was on Luc's other side, and he undid the leash tethering Luc's ankle to his board.

Iris screamed Luc's name, but he didn't respond. She desperately trailed Cal and Guillermo as they carried Luc to shore and lay him on the sand. Kelly announced that she had CPR training and, with complete authority, rolled Luc onto his back, tilting his chin up. She pinched his nose and started mouth-to-mouth resuscitation, alternating with chest compressions. Luc's chest rose and sank with Kelly's breaths. After several long moments, water gushed from Luc's mouth, and he sputtered. His eyes opened, and he clutched his arm.

"Thank God," Iris said.

Luc looked over at her and croaked, "Hey, babe. My arm. I think I broke it."

CHAPTER 13

Kelly gave Luc's arm a professional-looking inspection, gingerly probing it all over.

"Turn your arm from palm down to palm up," she instructed.

Luc winced at the effort and cradled his arm. "I can't. It hurts to move."

The rest of the surfing students gathered around Luc, watching nervously. Lisa grabbed a flowered scarf she'd brought to the beach and made a sling for him. She fastened it around his neck.

He carefully slipped his arm through the loop. "Ah, that helps. Thanks."

Cal was nearby, ending a muted conversation on his phone. "Come on, Luc. It's a half-hour drive to the hospital in Nicoya. They can do an x-ray there. And thank you, Kelly, for your expert help."

"Let me grab some clothes for him." Iris said. "I'm coming with you."

"Meet us at the parking lot," Cal called over his shoulder.

Iris ran to the cottage and grabbed a zippered fleece and sandals for Luc. She threw on a sundress over her bathing suit. After tossing his wallet into her purse, she scanned the room. Should she bring her muscle relaxer pills for him? Better stick with ibuprofen and a bottle of water.

By the time Iris reached the parking lot, she found Cal easing Luc into the front seat of a resort-branded jeep. Cal was trying to fit the shoulder belt around him without causing more pain. Someone had given Luc an ice pack, which he'd propped against his arm.

Once Luc was secured in his seat, Iris slipped the sandals on him and wrapped the jacket around his shoulders. She hopped into the back seat. "I brought ibuprofen and water. Do you want some?"

"Wait," Cal cautioned as he pulled out of the driveway. "You shouldn't eat or drink anything in case you need surgery."

"Can't I dry swallow some pills?" Luc asked. "I'd like some help with the pain."

"Just one pill. But no water. It's probably a simple break and the doctor will put on a cast, but an x-ray will confirm what you need." Cal turned onto a slightly wider, better-paved road and sped up.

Iris leaned forward from the back seat and handed Luc a pill. "Does it happen often, the waves suddenly getting so much bigger like that?"

"No. It's rare," Cal said. "But when a strong cold front passes to the north, powerful winds can funnel through the inland valley to smack into the ocean. That can add several feet to the underlying swell. I was monitoring the weather, and those big breaks weren't supposed to hit until this afternoon. I don't know what happened, but I apologize, Luc. You shouldn't have had to face such big waves on your third day of surfing."

Luc grunted, "Baptism by fire."

Was Cal worried that Luc might sue the resort? Management should have foreseen a dangerous situation which put their inexperienced students at risk. Not that she or Luc were litigious. Hopefully, the break wasn't too bad and would heal quickly. Still, the accident would ruin Luc's plan to spend the next two weeks perfecting his surfing. It wasn't fair.

After some time, simple stucco houses with metal roofs appeared alongside the road. The addition of gas stations and small strip malls indicated that they were approaching a town.

"Hospital La Anexion is about ten minutes up the road," Cal said. "Healthcare in Costa Rica is excellent, and this is where all the ex-pats go. The doctors speak pretty good English, but I'll be with you in case anything needs to be translated in more detail."

Luc had been silent for most of the ride, with his eyes closed and his lips tightly compressed. He looked like he was in a good deal of pain.

"Did the ibuprofen help?" Iris asked.

"A little," Luc said through gritted teeth.

Cal swung the jeep into the hospital driveway and parked in the shade of a palm tree. After they entered, Cal spoke quietly to the receptionist. A woman in navy scrubs led them up to an exam room on the second floor.

Luc's board shorts had dried out on the ride over. He sat on the elevated exam table and handed Iris the sling and fleece. His arm looked swollen. She and Cal took the visitor chairs. They didn't have to wait long before there was a knock on the door and a man in a white coat entered the room.

"Good afternoon, Mr. Cormier. I'm Doctor Juan Mora, an orthopedic specialist." He consulted Luc's chart. "I understand you've had a surfing accident, and you might have broken your arm. Let me look at what we have here, okay?"

Dr. Mora put Luc through essentially the same series of prods and pokes as Kelly had, then announced, "It looks like a simple fracture of the ulna in the forearm, but the bone seems to be a little out of alignment. We'll find out more from the x-rays. We may have to re-align the bones in the ER and apply a plaster cast. This will take some time. Your friends can wait downstairs in the cafeteria, and someone will come find them when you're ready to go home."

The cafeteria in the basement turned out to be pleasant enough, with high windows overlooking the parking lot and a lush tropical garden beyond. Iris and Cal got cups of strong coffee and sat at a window table. Despite her worried state, she marveled at how good the coffee was in this country, even in a hospital cafeteria.

"Guess we'll be here for a while," Iris said. Luc was in good hands to deal with his injury, but she was feeling increasingly annoyed with Cal that the accident had happened at all.

Cal looked at his watch, took out his phone, and stood up. "Excuse me, I need to step outside to make some calls."

She nodded. "I'll stay here in case there's news about Luc."

An hour later, Iris felt herself dozing off when she heard the squeak of the cafeteria doors opening. A nurse guided Luc in a wheelchair, his left arm now encased in a bulky white cast, elbow to wrist.

CHAPTER 14

Back at the casita, Iris followed Luc into the shower and helped him scrub the encrusted salt and sand off. The hospital had sent him home with a waterproof cover to put over his cast, but the process was still awkward, and he winced from pain every time he moved his arm.

"Too bad there's no tub in here," Iris said while carefully toweling him off.

"I can't believe this happened. I'm so bummed out."

"Do you want to cut our trip short and go back to Cambridge? Surfing together was the whole reason we came." She waited for his answer, wondering which response she was hoping for.

"No way." Luc clumsily tried to use a hair dryer with his uninjured right arm. "It's beautiful here, and you can still surf without me. I'll spend some time feeling sorry for myself, then probably find things to keep me busy. Maybe I'll hang out with Chef Vargas."

"I bet he'd love having a curious interloper in his kitchen as much as you would in yours."

"Yeah, maybe you're right." Luc searched one-handed through the closet for a shirt that would be easy to pull on. He slid a black polo shirt over the cast, then got it stuck between his elbow and his head.

Iris heard his muffled curses and hurried over to pull the shirt down into place.

"Damn, I *hate* being helpless!" he exclaimed.

"I know. It sucks." Was she about to see a new side of her lover? Her ex-husband, Christopher, had been a first-class hypochondriac. In the two-plus years she and Luc had known each other, neither had come down with anything more serious than a cold. "It's almost time for New Year's Eve cocktails. Alcohol should ease the pain." Iris hesitated. "Wait—are you on any major meds now?"

"Yup. Tylenol with codeine. The doctor said mixing that with alcohol could cause huge problems. Could even kill me."

"So much for that idea."

Iris and Luc heard a sudden loud smack coming from the direction of their veranda and rushed out to find Julio, wearing a tool belt and positioning a ladder against the overhanging roof of their casita. A wheelbarrow filled with strips of Iris's anti-monkey guards sat nearby.

"Sorry to disturb you," Julio said. "Ms. Winters asked me to install these on the roofs of the casitas. Is that okay? My screw gun might make a little noise."

Iris walked over to the wheelbarrow and held up a section to show Luc. "Wow. They're built already. Pretty ingenious, right?"

"I'll say. The monkeys have a choice to either impale themselves or go elsewhere. I hope they choose option B." Luc gave Julio a loose salute. "I'll leave you to it." He headed inside, awkwardly swiveling through the door to avoid hitting his cast.

Iris stayed out on the veranda. "Did you build all of these?" At Julio's nod, she said, "I only drew up the sketch yesterday. You're a fast carpenter."

A flush crept over his cheeks. "The design is very smart. Ms. Winters said that you are an architect."

She studied a piece of wood with bamboo spikes. "I am. And it looks like you followed my sketch exactly. Thank you. Let's find out if it works."

Julio grabbed a few of the strips and headed up the ladder. Iris followed him and sat down carefully on the thatch. Julio squatted, ready to work. He took a piece of paper out of his jeans' pocket, unfolded it and read the dimensions listed. "Your sketch says to place these six inches apart. I think that's about fifteen centimeters, no? Then

I screw them into the ceiling joists. But I'll have to avoid hitting the hurricane straps along the eaves and at the beams."

"Aren't you south of the usual hurricane path here?" Iris asked.

Julio reached in his tool belt for a long piece of stiff wire for locating the rafters through the thatch. "Generally, yes, but we still have to build for the occasional ones that blow through."

"You seem to know a lot about construction."

Julio sat back on his heels and looked up. "I want to be an architect."

"That's great. What do you have to do to get your professional qualification?"

Julio rolled his eyes. "It takes forever. Six years total to get your Master of Architecture. I passed my tests and am waiting to hear from the Escuela de Arquitectura outside of San José to see if they will offer me a scholarship."

"It's a long process for architecture school everywhere."

Julio located two rafters and placed a section of the guard between them. "But I have responsibilities here. I need to help my relatives. I don't know if I can leave them to go study." His large eyes looked so defeated. "Maybe it's only a dream."

"No, you should do it!" Iris objected. "Maybe the Winters can help your family here. You can't give up on your dream!" They sat silently for a moment, and it felt like something intangible passed between them. A psychic nudge perhaps.

Then Iris heard the casita door below opening and Luc's upturned face appeared beyond the veranda roof.

"Iris, we should get dressed now for the big shindig. I need your help."

She rested a hand on Julio's arm. "I'm serious. Find a way to make your dream happen." Then she climbed down the ladder.

CHAPTER 15

Iris and Luc were running late for the celebration because it took a long time for him to dress. Iris helped him into a loose white shirt, rolling up one sleeve, and draped his tan linen jacket over his shoulders to accommodate his sling. She wore a long tight red dress with a low (for her) neckline. She added a pair of dangly gold earrings and a white jacket.

They could hear the distinctive beat of calypso music as they strolled over to the beach. Cal and Sierra met them at the cove entrance, now marked with a flower-covered arch made from interwoven branches.

Cal eyed Luc thoughtfully. "How are you feeling?"

"A little tired." Luc admitted. "I doubt I'll make it 'til midnight to see in the new year."

"Don't you worry about that," Sierra said. "Enjoy the evening and turn in whenever you want."

"It looks beautiful!" Iris said. "Happy New Year."

The cove resembled a magical fairyland. Tall torches sunk into the sand cast flickering shadows, tablecloths flapped in the breeze, and candles flickered inside hurricane lamps. The yoga platform had been brought over to use as a dance floor. A live band was set up in the middle.

The other guests all noticed Iris and Luc's arrival, and he immediately became the center of attention.

"Was it a simple break?" Kelly asked.

"I don't know how simple it was," he answered. "They had to reset the bone. Something about the ulna. I was pretty out of it."

Iris asked Kelly, "How did you get your medical training? You were impressive. Didn't I hear you studied vineyard-management at college?"

Kelly laughed. "I learned emergency first-aid lifeguarding in the summers during high school. It's come in handy a few times."

"Can I sign your cast?" Eric called out.

"What is this, middle school?" Luc replied. "No one's signing this cast. I'll still be wearing it when I get back to my restaurant."

Eric stuck out his bottom lip in exaggerated disappointment. "But I had a nice sketch all worked out."

Tia rapped on Luc's cast gently with her finger. "Poor baby. I'm so sorry this happened. Did they at least give you some interesting meds at the hospital?"

Before he could answer, Margo swanned over, holding out two full cocktail glasses. "Mojitos for our fallen soldier and his trusty aide." Kenneth stood behind her, giving Luc a drunken grin.

Luc raised a hand. "Thanks, but I can't have anything hard with the painkillers they put me on. Iris will have to drink for me tonight." He glanced around, looking a little shaky. "And I think I need to sit now."

Iris steered him to a table and set down the glasses. "Do you want anything? Club soda, juice, Shirley Temple?"

He leaned back in his seat and closed his eyes. "No thanks. Think I'll just listen to the band. You know, they're pretty good."

Iris looked over at the four musicians and their unusual array of instruments. An acoustic guitar was the only one that looked familiar. Next to the guitarist, a man held a large bamboo stick upright like a string bass and whacked it expertly with a length of polished wood. The female percussionist pounded out a syncopated counter-rhythm on steel drums. The fourth musician shook a tambourine-looking contraption and crooned into a microphone in Spanish.

Margo, packaged into a tight sparkly dress, was out on the dance floor, shimmying to the music. Kenneth was circling around her, churning his arms like bicycle wheels. Tonight, he wore a leather vest over his untucked navy shirt and white jeans.

Cal and Sierra offered more professional moves, with coordinated wiggling of their hips and shoulders, interspersed with theatrical turns.

Lisa and Kelly stood on the far side of the band, sipping cocktails with fruit garnishes. Nearby, Tia gyrated subtly with both her arms out, trying to coax a clearly reluctant Eric to get up and dance.

Just as Luc was beginning to relax, Margo swooped in, grabbed Luc's uninjured hand, and pulled him up onto the dance floor. He shot Iris an imploring look, but she made a sweeping go-for-it gesture. She loved watching him dance, but before she could get comfortable, Kenneth pulled her into the middle of the swirl of bodies.

Iris had no trouble moving to the pulsing rhythm. But when the band started up with an energetic new song, Kenneth started swinging his arms like he was directing an airplane to its landing gate. Iris unintentionally burst out laughing. She positioned herself so she could watch Luc's sexy moves, his cast only slightly encumbering him. Margo seemed to appreciate his dancing style and placed her hands on either side of his hips. He jumped back. Iris quickly danced over and rested her own hand on Luc's shoulder to turn him around, effectively cutting in. "My patient needs to rest now," she explained to Margo, leading Luc back to their table.

Margo shrugged and turned toward Kenneth, who was bobbing his head in time to the music and snapping his fingers, looking lewdly at his girlfriend.

"Thanks for rescuing me," Luc said. "What is with that woman? Is she hyper sexed, or what?"

"Yup," Iris said. "And Kenneth seems to get off on watching her put the moves on other men."

"I guess we're not in New England anymore."

Between songs, they could hear the tide slapping against the sand. The effect was hypnotic. The upbeat music, a moon almost full, and the exotic scent of the flowers on the table intermingled with the smell of sea spray.

Until a foul odor overpowered everything. Iris looked around. At the next table, Kenneth twisted a fat cigar between his fingers. He lifted it to his lips and drew in a lungful of smoke, then let it out, the breeze carrying the stink in Iris and Luc's direction. Margo was meanwhile laughing at some undoubtedly unfunny comment he had made. *That woman is either drunk or an idiot. Or both.*

Kenneth noticed Iris's scowl and shouted, "What? We're outdoors!"

Iris and Luc signaled to the wait staff and moved to a table upwind. Luc muttered, "How can anyone appreciate good food after smoking a damn cigar? At least he could wait until after dessert."

Iris downed her second Mojito and tried to recapture the chill New Year's Eve mood she'd felt earlier. But her mind drifted back to the afternoon's rooftop conversation with Julio, and she remembered the warning she had overheard on Sunday about Julio doing something dangerous. At least she thought that was what the man had said. Julio seemed like a good person. *Should I warn Cal or Sierra about some danger he might be in? No, I'd better stay out of other people's business.*

The band switched over to a tango beat and the volume cranked up a notch. Soon everyone was swaying to the rhythm, or at least happily tapping their feet. Sierra and Cal broke into full dance mode, performing an expert tango with sweeping turns, intense eye contact, step-overs and a dramatic backfall ending. They had no inhibitions about everyone watching them. At the end of the song, the four seated couples clapped enthusiastically, and Margo hooted.

At that point, the pre-dinner set was over, and the musicians left the platform to take a break. Sierra stopped by Iris and Luc's table, not even slightly out of breath. "Isn't this band great? They rotate weekly between four of the nearby villages, and everyone gathers to dance in the town squares."

"You guys looked like professional dancers out there," Luc said.

"Dancing is a big, traditional part of the culture in Central America," Cal said.

Iris noticed several of the wait staff passing through the arch and approaching the tables, each carrying trays filled with plates of colorful appetizers.

"I hope you two are hungry." Sierra said. "Chef Vargas has prepared quite a feast."

"I'm starving," Luc said. "Eating seems to be the only thing I'm allowed to do. Thank God I didn't break my right arm or Iris would have to feed me by hand."

CHAPTER 16

The next morning, Luc felt grateful that he hadn't been able to drink the night before after witnessing Iris wake up groaning, holding her head in both hands, and staggering to the bathroom to down a handful of ibuprofens. And he'd been able to fully appreciate the nuances of the five-course meal Santiago Vargas had served them. He needed to learn what Santiago had used to glaze that duck. What was that sublime combination of spices? And who would have guessed that coconut could be combined with depigmented seaweed to create such an ambrosial dessert? God, the guy had chops.

They'd ended up leaving the party soon after the meal ended, two hours shy of midnight. It had been a long day.

At breakfast, the other guests also looked rough. They slugged back coffee and nibbled on toast, no one talking much. Nevertheless, at nine o'clock, the surfing students dutifully filed off to the beach for their next lesson.

Luc tried to cheer up as he headed in the opposite direction, back to the casita. He picked up the dense Cormac McCarthy novel he'd left face down on the veranda table and clambered into the hammock. Even with his strong meds, he'd spent the night thrashing around in bed, trying to find a comfortable position to sleep in, with no luck. His eyes felt heavy. He tented the book on his chest, rested his head back on a pillow, and dozed off.

When he awoke some time later, his watch read eleven o'clock, and he could see tiny surfers bobbing around in the distant swells. He lifted the binoculars Tia had loaned him at breakfast and adjusted the focus so he could see everyone clearly. Locating Iris, he watched her get to a wobbly standing position and ride a small wave in toward the beach. She had improved today, despite her epic hangover. He wanted her to catch the surfing bug so they could have an activity to share. He'd need to take some lessons at home to build on the brief sessions that his accident had interrupted. At this rate, he wouldn't be able to keep up with Iris.

Despite the heavy, uncomfortable cast, Luc felt antsy. How could he get some exercise? His left arm was worse than useless, but his legs still worked. Luc went inside to change from his shorts into a bathing suit. Wrestling into it one-handed was exercise in itself. He popped another couple of ibuprofens, put on a baseball cap, and headed over to the pool.

Margo had arrayed herself on a chaise lounge under an umbrella, reading a glossy magazine. She looked up and lowered her sunglasses. "Well, hello. Have you come to keep me company? There's not even a pool boy here today, and Sammy the bartender has only been around once."

"I can get you something from the pavilion if you'd like."

"No, honey. I should wait on you. You're injured. Anything *you* need?"

"Uh, I'm fine, thanks."

Luc tugged the waterproof cover up over his cast and headed down the steps into the shallow end of the pool. He strode across the width of the pool, using the water to create some resistance. He felt ridiculous, but at least he was getting a bit of a workout. After twenty minutes, he climbed back out of the pool and collected a towel from the grass hut. He spread it out on a chaise near Margo, took his cast cover off, and lay down.

She took this as an invitation to chat. "So, how long have you and Iris been together?"

"Two and a half years. How about you and Kenneth?"

"Ken dropped by my gallery in Houston to pick up a gift last year and we hit it off, so I guess we're still in the honeymoon stage." She giggled.

Luc looked over at the woman, sunbathing in full make-up, with painted nails like talons. He tried to picture her as a business owner. What kind of business, exactly?

"You know, with your arm in a cast, you need to keep your blood circulating so your muscles don't shrivel up. I'd recommend getting a massage. Unfortunately, Sierra said their masseuse just left the resort. She's looking for a new one, but I guess it's hard to get good help around here."

"That's okay. The doctor gave me some exercises to do."

Margo looked at him slyly. "If you're interested, I've been told I give a pretty good massage." She winked.

"Thanks. I'm good," Luc answered hurriedly, and snapped open his book to emphasize the point.

At lunch, Kelly and Lisa asked Iris and Luc if they could join their table. All agreed, they proceeded to fill their plates at the buffet table.

"Mateo told me you two went into Santa Elena with him yesterday." Kelly set her plate down on the placemat. "What did you think of the village?"

"Very authentic, not someplace dressed up and geared toward tourists." Luc stacked his tray on top of the others. "We like exploring places like that."

"We bought some nice bowls at a pottery studio that belongs to Mateo's sister," Iris added.

"Isn't there a museum in that village?" Lisa asked. "Did you check that out?"

"Yeah. It's tiny," Iris said, "but it had some interesting old pottery. Its prized artifact is this amazing clay crocodile sitting on top of an urn. It has a huge emerald tear that makes it look like it's crying."

"Cool, I'd love to see that." Kelly turned to her mother. "Santa Elena—that's where the orphanage is, right? The one that Cal and Sierra support."

Lisa nodded.

"Is it?" Iris said. "I wish we had gone to see it."

"I'm surprised that Mateo didn't mention the place. He grew up there," Kelly said. "Mom and I are thinking of driving over there this afternoon. We have a car and you're welcome to join us. We might sponsor an internship at our winery for any of the older kids who might be interested. But I guess we should run that idea by Cal and Sierra first."

Luc looked at Iris, who said. "Sure, we'd love to go with you. I think Sierra told us that Ana, the masseuse, and her cousin, Julio, also grew up there, but she didn't mention Mateo. I guess a lot of the staff here are connected to that orphanage."

"Yes, Cal and Sierra have been so supportive of the people in the area. Driving here from San José, the Ticos we've met have been universally kind." Lisa said. "We tried to take the scenic route but managed to hit some pretty primitive back roads. At one point, our GPS led us straight to a river's edge. A sign there told us we had to call a certain cell phone number in order to get across. Ten minutes later, a local guy drove up and charged us 10,000 colones to get into our Jeep and drive it across the fast-moving current. I'm not sure how he got back to the other side."

"Hmm. Sounds like a racket set up with the GPS operator," Luc said.

Lisa laughed. "Well, that worked out to about twenty dollars. We looked on a map later and there was a land route around the peninsula, but it was much longer, so the shakedown was probably worth it."

"We love poking around in places off the tourist trail," Kelly said.

"And seeing special things—like that crying crocodile." Lisa said. "Do you think the museum will be open on New Year's Day?"

"Let's find out," Iris said.

CHAPTER 17

After lunch, Iris and Luc walked over to Lisa and Kelly's casita to join them for the visit to the orphanage. They followed the Duvals to the parking lot.

Iris was relieved to see that their vehicle was a jeep. "Now this is the kind of car you need on the roads out here," she said. "My brain was getting jiggled around in Mateo's sedan on Monday. I kept hitting my head on the roof."

Kelly settled quickly into the driver's seat and gestured for Luc to sit next to her in front to accommodate his long legs, not to mention the bulky cast on his arm.

Lisa and Iris slid into the back.

With the car's air conditioning on and functioning shock absorbers to cushion the bumps, the time it took for them to reach Santa Elena seemed a lot shorter today. Iris recognized some landmarks as they approached the village.

The Jeep's GPS directed them reasonably close to a three-story concrete building with an orange metal roof, two blocks from Santa Elena's central plaza. Kelly parked on the street and consulted a crumpled piece of paper pulled from her pocket. "Sierra told us to check in with a Señora Maria Ramos who runs the place and said she would give us a tour. I wonder if I should have called first."

"I wish Luc and I spoke Spanish," Iris said. "I hate to expect locals to defer to us and speak English."

"Don't worry. Mom and I can translate," Kelly said.

A rusty front gate creaked open at Lisa's push. The other three followed her across a scrabbly, weed-strewn lawn to the front door. There was no doorbell, so Lisa knocked. They waited a while in the hot sun. Luc tentatively tried the knob, and the door opened.

"Not very good security," Lisa said.

"Maybe there's no crime to worry about," Kelly said. "I guess we can go in."

It was cooler inside the dim entrance, but no more charming. There was no receptionist or obvious management office, only a vestibule with peeling paint and a long hallway in front of them. They smelled cooked carrots and something sulfuric. The foursome approached the first doorway, which was cracked partway open. Kelly knocked on the doorframe as they peeked in.

Iris was surprised to see Violetta sitting in front of a large computer monitor, her fingers flying over the keyboard. But her waist-long hair had been drastically cut into a short pixie.

"Esperar," Violetta called over her shoulder.

"Violetta," Iris blurted out. "You cut your hair."

The woman spun around in her chair, her brows rising in alarm as she took in the strangers. "Yo no soy Violetta. I'm the sister, Veronica. How-do-you-say… gemela?"

"Twin," Kelly translated. "Disculpe. ¿Sabes dónde es Señora Ramos?"

"No sé."

"We should have called first," Lisa muttered. "¿Alguien puede darnos un recorrido por el orfanato?" Lisa turned to Iris and Luc. "She doesn't know where Señora Ramos is, but I asked if someone could give us a tour of the orphanage."

Veronica held up a finger. "Un momento."

Iris saw a bed in the far corner of the small room, neatly covered with a cotton bedspread. They were invading the poor woman's bedroom. "We should wait in the hall," she whispered.

They backed out and stood in the hall, wondering if Veronica meant to join them or would call someone else to show them around. The hallway's stucco walls were a depressing gray, and all the doors looked weathered. This building needed an infusion of cash. Maybe Sierra and Cal focused on investing in teaching the children skills before paying for upgrades to the infrastructure.

A few minutes later, Veronica emerged and gave them a tentative smile. "Is okay. I do the tour."

"That would be great," Lisa said. "Thank you."

They followed her, the sound of their sandals slapping on the concrete floor. Veronica guided them first to a nursery where four babies were lying on their backs or crawling around inside a playpen. A teenage boy sat on a stool next to the enclosure studying his phone rather than attending to the babies. He put the device down as soon as he saw the visitors. He quickly scooped up a crying baby and took it over to a changing table to put on a clean diaper.

Iris caught Luc's eye. His shrug told her they were thinking the same thing: this orphanage was not a shining example of enlightened child-raising.

The next stops were equally unimpressive. Some middle-schoolers were playing stickball in the courtyard unsupervised. Veronica led them into a room with a double row of identical little beds, straight out of Charles Dickens. The group located the source of the prevalent odors when they entered a tiny kitchen where a gray-haired woman was stirring a large pot of beans. And finally, they passed an alcove with three teenagers lined up waiting for a fourth one to finish her turn on an old desktop computer.

"How many children live here?" Luc asked.

Veronica thought for a moment. "Twenty," then waffled her right hand back and forth to suggest "about."

They had looped around each of the building's two stories and were back at the front vestibule. They thanked Veronica for their whistle-stop tour and headed back to the Jeep.

"Well, that was depressing," Kelly said. "I have a feeling we would have seen an edited, cleaned-up version if we had alerted Señora Ramos ahead of time that we were coming."

"To be fair," Lisa said, "we don't know what kind of life these kids would have had if they weren't here in the orphanage. They might have been living on the street, panhandling, or worse."

"True," Luc agreed. "I think I'll ask Sierra how we can contribute to make the place better—more teachers, a coat of paint, maybe more computers. She'll probably know what they need most."

"And we can run a benefit for them at the winery," Kelly looked at her mother, who nodded.

They had arrived back at the jeep.

"Anyone up for ice cream? Our treat," Iris said. "We saw a shop on the plaza yesterday."

On their walk over, Iris noticed several clusters of villagers gathered on the sidewalk talking excitedly. "I don't remember so many people milling around yesterday."

"It's New Year's Day, a holiday from work," Kelly said as they headed toward the shop.

"I keep forgetting that this is a new year," Iris said. "I've totally lost track of what day it is."

"That's the sign of a good vacation," Luc said.

A small line had formed in front of the takeout window. They chose flavors, and each received a plastic cup. Iris tossed the coins she received as change into her daypack pocket. The ice cream turned out to be shaved ice with condensed milk, more like a gravelly milkshake. Iris's flavor was a delicious coconut with raspberry syrup. They sipped their shakes and sucked on the ice as they strolled around the plaza under the fragrant frangipani trees.

"There's the museum we visited yesterday." Iris pointed. "Do you want to see the crying crocodile?"

"Absolutely," Kelly said. "You wouldn't mind skipping yoga today, would you, Mom?"

"To see a crying crocodile? I'm sold."

But as they crossed the plaza, they saw a white car parked askew out front with POLICIA written on the side. Two men in black uniforms were conferring at the top of the stairs, with a banner of yellow crime scene tape strung across the closed door.

The group climbed a few steps and Kelly asked the officers, "¿Está todo bien?"

The older police officer looked at her suspiciously. "¿Qué está haciendo aquí?"

Lisa translated for Iris and Luc the man's question about what they were doing there.

"Nosotros queremos visitar el museo," Kelly answered.

"El museo esta cerrado. Hubo un robo y un asesintato."

Kelly took a step back. "Un robo y asesinato?"

"Sí. Anoche la cocodrilo llorando urna fue robada y el vigilante nocturno fue asesinado."

Kelly's face fell, and she turned to face the others. "Last night, the crying crocodile urn was stolen, and the thief murdered the museum's night watchman!"

CHAPTER 18

On the long, bumpy ride back to the resort, Iris filled the Duvals in on the story behind the jade pieces and how, now, they had all four been systematically stolen within the last two weeks.

"But after the first break-in, certainly after the second, wouldn't the museums have known the thieves were coming? Couldn't they have stepped up their security or moved the urns somewhere else for the time being?" Lisa asked.

"Maybe they did that, but it wasn't enough," Luc suggested. "The watchman was probably added for extra night-time security, but on Monday, it looked like the only one guarding the urn during the day was a frail old lady."

For a few moments, they were all silent.

"I took some photos of the Crying Crocodile yesterday." Iris fumbled for her phone in the pocket of her shorts. "Here, let me show you what it looks like."

From the driver's seat, Kelly glanced at the phone as Luc held it out. "It's really ancient," she said.

"From about 500 BCE," Luc said.

When it was Lisa's turn to admire the image, she mused, "Imagine the artist who carved this, never guessing his work would endure, connecting him to people over two thousand years later." She handed the phone back to Iris. "Is that enormous emerald real? It must be very valuable."

"Each of the four pieces has a different gemstone, all of them worth a fortune," Iris explained. "But the fact that they're some of the few artifacts from that period makes them historically important for Costa Rica. The natives living here then were not Mayan, Inca, or Aztec. Not much is known about them. These artifacts were a rare link to their culture."

On his phone, Luc found the latest update on the Tica Times website. He skimmed it. "This article doesn't tell us anything new. The thieves shot the guard, a nineteen-year-old young man from the village and bypassed the alarm system like before. The urn was the only thing they took."

"Maybe I'm being naïve," Lisa said, "but I can't believe any of the local Ticos would be cold-blooded enough to murder a local kid and steal such culturally important artifacts."

"I've read about international antiquity looting rings. I doubt that whoever's behind this would stop at murder to steal a collection like this," Luc said.

Lisa sighed. "Wouldn't it be incredible if we had some way to help track down whoever did this?"

"Mom and I are addicted to TV crime shows and podcasts," Kelly explained.

Luc's eyes found Iris's in the rear-view mirror and rested there a few beats. She looked away. He was always warning her to avoid getting mixed up in dangerous intrigues. There was no way she was going near this minefield on her vacation.

CHAPTER 19

Once Iris and Luc had made their way back to their casita, she collapsed on the bed, feeling light-headed. "Between surfing this morning and trudging around Santa Elena in the heat, I'm exhausted. I feel like ordering room service for dinner and curling up with a book."

"We don't have to stay long in the pavilion. I'm kind of tired too." Luc dropped onto the bed beside her. "But I'd like to hear Sierra and Cal's take on the news about these thefts. Living here, they would need to keep up with the local happenings."

Iris thought for a moment. "I guess I'm curious about that, too. Give me a few minutes. I'll take a shower and maybe that will give me a second wind."

Luc retrieved the waterproof cover for his cast and followed her into the bathroom.

An hour later, they entered the pavilion to the sound of reggae music coming over the speakers. Margo was the only one out on the dance floor. Kenneth sat at a table, scowling into his phone as the other guests stood around chatting. Iris and Luc took in the scene and headed for the bar.

Iris ordered a piña colada from Sammy, and Luc immediately decided to have the same.

"That's right," said Iris. "You're done with your meds. You can drink again! How's the arm feeling?"

"Not bad. Although it's starting to itch under the cast."

"I can give you the perfect essential oil to drizzle down inside it," Sierra offered, sliding up behind them. The woman was stealthy as a cat. "It will take care of the dry skin."

"Uh," Luc said, looking startled. "That would be… great. Thanks."

Cal then joined them. There was a sense of compressed energy about the man, so different from his wife's Zen-like chill. Iris made a conscious effort to avoid staring at the prominent scar on his face.

"A Papagayo Ale, Sammy, and…" Cal turned to Sierra. "A Chardonnay, dear?" She nodded. Sammy reached down to an under-counter cooler, keeping his eyes on the room.

"I hear you visited the orphanage this afternoon. What did you think of it?" Cal asked, looking past them at Margo.

"We weren't able to connect with Señora Ramos, but Veronica gave us a nice tour," Iris said. "I didn't realize they had babies there, too."

"Yes, but most of them aren't really orphans." Sierra's voice was sad. "Their parents or, more commonly, their unwed mothers abandoned them. People in the surrounding villages know that the orphanage will take them in, no questions asked."

"It must take a lot of resources to clothe and feed everyone, much less provide them with schooling," Luc said.

"It does," Cal agreed. "We were able to buy the building, but you probably noticed that it still needs a lot of work."

"Iris and I and the Duvals would like to host some benefits at our businesses back home to help," Luc said.

"That would be most welcome. We do need to develop a broader support network." Sierra smiled. The music stopped, and everyone swiveled their heads around to locate a table.

Sierra patted Luc's uninjured arm. "We can discuss this later."

Before Sierra and Cal could turn away, Iris brought up a new topic. "After our tour, we tried to show the Duvals the little museum in Santa Elena, but thieves had just broken in. They killed the night watchman and stole their prized exhibit."

Cal's face froze, and his eyes narrowed. When he spoke, his voice was a low growl. "The bastards shot Julio and made off with the last of the quartet!"

Iris sucked in a breath. "Julio? Not the young man who works here?"

"Yes, our Julio." Sierra's voice wavered. "The police came and told us about it this afternoon. I'm heartsick. He took the night watchman job at the museum to earn extra money. He was saving up for architecture school. The nicest kid…"

Cal added, "And Julio's cousin, Ana, has disappeared. We have no way of knowing if she's okay."

"Ana, the masseuse?" Iris asked.

Sierra nodded, and a tear rolled down her cheek.

Cal put his arm around Sierra. "We should go home. It's been an upsetting day." They excused themselves and headed out of the pavilion.

Luc turned to Iris. "Wasn't Julio the guy putting those monkey guards on the roof yesterday?"

"Yes, that was him and we talked about his dream of going to architecture school. That was just last night! He must have gone to the museum job right afterward." Iris felt a chill run through her. "And why is Ana missing?"

They walked over to their table and sank into their seats.

Iris stared at Luc blankly. "I can't believe Julio is dead!"

CHAPTER 20

The next morning at breakfast, Cal made an announcement: After lunch, Guillermo and Mateo would lead an expedition through the rain forest to visit waterfalls and hot springs for any of the guests who were interested. He cautioned that, after a forty-minute drive, there would be an easy half-hour hike to and from the spot, so everyone should wear sturdy shoes. As he said that, he looked directly at Margo. He asked them to assemble at the pavilion entrance at one-thirty and to bring bathing suits, towels, and bug spray. Mateo and Guillermo would meet them there with the van.

Everyone was enthusiastic at the prospect of a field trip, even Margo. As the initial excitement subsided, Sierra approached Luc at their table. "Cal and I feel so bad that you aren't able to take advantage of the surfing classes anymore, so we want to make sure that you have enough to keep you busy. I'm glad you're going on the waterfall excursion. It's quite a magnificent spot. But please know that if you two would prefer to leave early, we could reschedule your trip for another time, after your arm has a chance to heal."

Luc's eyebrows rose. "Actually, this is the first vacation either of us has been able to fit into our crazy schedules in years. But I'm enjoying being here and relaxing. And, at the rate Iris's surfing is improving, she will be giving me lessons when we get back to Massachusetts."

Iris flashed him an amused half-smile, imagining that situation.

"Well, good," Sierra said. "And I can arrange more excursions in the afternoons. Let me know if there's anything you particularly want to see—a coffee plantation or a volcano, perhaps."

"Sure," Luc said.

"Excellent." Sierra turned and, with her conspicuously perfect yogini posture, glided over to where Cal was chatting with Lisa and Kelly.

Iris and Luc waited at the pavilion entrance at one-thirty as the others joined them.

On hearing the crunching sound of tires on pea stone, they all looked up. The same white resort van that had greeted them at the airstrip pulled up and Mateo and Guillermo stepped out.

"Ready to see some amazing sights?" Guillermo smiled broadly.

Margo and Kenneth wore matching khaki safari outfits—canvas fedoras, cuffed shorts, and shirts with multiple pockets and epaulets.

Tia murmured to Iris, "How did we miss the *Indiana Jones* memo?"

Lisa and Kelly were the last to appear, wearing their usual shorts and T-shirts. Everyone gravitated toward the same seats they had chosen five days before, with the Duvals climbing into the uncomfortable back row.

Mateo twisted around from the driver's seat. "We have a forty-minute drive ahead of us along the coastline to reach the trailhead. There are plenty of cold water bottles up here if anyone is thirsty." Guillermo passed back a few bottles to those who signaled for them.

"Is there a bathroom there?" Margo asked. "I hate peeing in the woods, although I will if I have to."

"There's a very basic bathroom and changing rooms near the waterfall," Guillermo assured her.

Mateo started the van, and they bounced along the rutted road, soon catching views of the vast ocean off to their left. Iris opened her window for some fresh air because the smell of everyone's bug spray was overpowering. But the dust kicking up from the road made her sneeze, so she shut it again.

After what seemed like a long time, they reached a small clearing off the side of the road, and Mateo wedged the van in between some bushes. No other cars were in sight. The two guides slipped on backpacks as everyone else got out and adjusted their binoculars, sunglasses, and other paraphernalia.

Guillermo said, "December is considered the beginning of the dry season in Costa Rica, but, as you can see, the forest remains very green. You'll have an easier time spotting animals now because the vegetation is slightly less lush than during the wet season from May through November. This part of the rainforest is off the beaten path, so we probably won't encounter any other visitors."

"Are there snakes here? Dangerous snakes?" Margo interrupted.

"Sure. We have fer-de-lances, eyelash vipers, green vine snakes, coral snakes, jumping pit vipers, and, oh yes, boa constrictors," Mateo said with a relish. He shrugged. "And probably more. This is the jungle."

Margo gasped and theatrically clutched Kenneth's arm.

Guillermo glared at Mateo and said, "Keep to the path and you'll be fine. It's cool out and snakes go into a low-energy state in the winter. You'll rarely see them unless you're seriously poking around. Let's start walking. I'll point out some birds, animals, and plants, but you should ask me about anything that interests you. It's about a half-hour walk to the waterfalls and the hot springs. Mateo will bring up the rear."

CHAPTER 21

As the group left the clearing and moved into the forest, tall trees blocked much of the sunlight, and it was too dark for sunglasses. Iris could hear the buzz of insects, the random chirping of birds, and vague rustling noises seemingly everywhere.

"What are these trees with the sinewy trunks?" she asked. "It looks like the roots are lifting out of the ground."

Guillermo rested his hand on one of the big fibrous offshoots. "These are actually woody liana vines. They wrap around the trees and climb up to reach the sunlight at the canopy. We're only beginning to learn about the complicated role they play in photosynthesis and in storing water and carbon."

Most of the guests took out their phones to photograph Guillermo next to the immense vines. The humid air smelled earthy, like decaying vegetation. Just then, there was rustling overhead, and they heard some deep, growling sounds. Everyone looked up and held their camera phones at the ready.

"A group of white-faced capuchins are coming through. These are even more common than howler monkeys," Mateo said. There was a chorus of artificial shutter sounds.

Eric pinch-enlarged the image on his phone. "Their teeth look pretty sharp. Are they aggressive?"

"They can be. But they'll stay up near the canopy and not bother us," Mateo answered.

After the group had continued down the narrow path for a long fifteen minutes, Lisa asked, "What are those iridescent blue butterflies? They're gorgeous."

Guillermo caught one gently in his hands, showed it carefully to everyone, then let it go. "That's the Blue Morpho, Costa Rica's national butterfly. We have thirteen hundred different species of butterflies here, but the Blue Morpho is the most famous."

They walked on, deep into the rainforest, stopping to take pictures and point out various exotic things to their companions.

Iris leaned close to Luc. "How does your arm feel?"

"The sling helps, but I think I need to take more ibuprofen when we get to the waterfall."

Ten minutes further on, Kenneth stopped, and the line behind him was brought to a sudden halt. He pointed a thick forefinger at a brightly colored red, blue and yellow bird up in a tree. "Is that a macaw, Guillermo, or a parrot? How do you tell them apart?"

Iris caught sight of the enormous bird almost three feet long. It had wavy black lines on its face and its colors positively glowed.

Guillermo answered, "It's a Macaw, the largest type of parrot in the world. They have longer tails than other parrots and white skin on their faces instead of feathers. They're highly intelligent and social."

"Beautiful!" Kelly said, capturing the bird on video as it flew off. "I hope it's not endangered."

"Not in Costa Rica," Guillermo assured her.

They moved along and Iris heard the far-away sound of rushing water.

"Is that the waterfall I hear?" Eric called out. "It sounds big."

"Up ahead," Mateo said.

The roar of the cascade grew louder, and as they rounded a corner, the group looked up to see a frothy torrent rushing over rocks and landing a hundred feet down in a deep, natural pool. A cloud of mist hovered above it. The pond was surrounded by lush green jungle and looked pre-historic.

"Wow," was all Iris could say.

"This is a serious waterfall," Kelly said. "It's spectacular. I'm surprised it's not packed with tourists."

"We try to keep this place a secret, for small groups only." Mateo said. "Most tourists go to the larger falls at the Parque Nacional in Rincón. Still, we're lucky to have it all to ourselves today."

Guillermo pointed out the two small buildings which offered some privacy and rudimentary bathrooms. The women and men separated to change into their bathing suits.

When Iris emerged, she found Luc sitting on a log, struggling to stretch the waterproof cover over his cast.

"Here, let me help," she said.

"Hey, is that a condom for your arm?" Eric chuckled as Tia gave him a disgusted look. Eric took a running jump into the clear water, then let out a shriek. "It's cold!"

Guillermo gestured to the three terraced pools surrounded by rocks off to one side. "Those are the hot springs. You can relax in those first, then cool off in the swimming hole. But don't stay too long at a time in the springs or you'll overheat."

Iris dipped her toes into the pool, and it felt refreshing after their long hike. She continued in further and knelt to completely immerse herself. "It's not really so cold."

Kelly and Lisa followed her in.

Luc climbed up on the rocks to the lowest of the hot springs and slid his legs in, keeping his injured arm out of the water. Iris soon joined him. The others spread out among the three levels of hot springs, the water warm but strangely soothing in the jungle heat.

Iris lay next to Luc, with her head resting against a smooth stone. She closed her eyes.

"This is paradise, isn't it?" Luc said.

She looked over at him, his head thrown back to face the sunlight. She was relieved that his disappointment at missing out on surfing didn't seem to be spoiling his time here. "It is," she said. "Hey, look at that." A foot-long iguana, almost perfectly camouflaged against the rocks, was sunning itself next to Luc's propped-up cast.

He glanced at it and laughed. "We're definitely not in New England anymore."

Mateo and Guillermo were setting out refreshments down along the edge of the cold pool. Iris realized she was hungry. And, after twenty minutes, it was probably time to get out of the hot spring water. "I'm going to cool off and get something to eat."

Luc followed her carefully down the rocks. The guides had spread out banana bread, lemon curd cake, and watermelon juice on a blanket. They invited the guests to help themselves.

Margo asked Mateo, "Got any vodka to add to this juice? It needs a little something."

"Sorry, no, but back at the resort, of course," he answered.

"You don't need that," Kenneth frowned at Margo.

"That's a damn shame," Margo responded, pouring herself another cup of juice. "Those hot springs make me so thirsty."

"After you have finished your snacks, we'll stay here long enough for another quick dip before heading back," Guillermo said. "It's better not to be way out here when it starts to get dark."

CHAPTER 22

After the group had changed back into dry clothes, they set out on the dirt path back to the van. Margo walked up front with Guillermo while Kenneth kept to the rear. Iris wondered if there was some friction between them.

Thinking of romance, or the lack thereof, Iris remembered that she'd arranged with Sierra at the beginning of the trip to have dinner served tonight for her and Luc on their casita veranda under the expected full moon. But now, after Luc's accident, she wasn't sure if he'd be in any kind of romantic mood.

They'd been walking for about twenty minutes when Iris checked her watch. It was already four-thirty, and the sun would set in barely an hour. Being in the rainforest so close to dusk made her uneasy. Who knew what nocturnal predators would awaken? She wished they could walk faster, but everyone was casually admiring the flora and fauna, and asking the guides endless questions.

Eric bent down and ripped off some leaves from a stringy grass-like clump. "Hey, I didn't know this grew in the wild." He held it up to Luc, who sniffed it.

"Lemongrass." Luc said. "I've noticed that Chef Vargas uses it a lot."

Eric passed it to Tia to smell.

The light in the dark forest was getting dimmer and dimmer. Iris wondered if the guides had flashlights in their backpacks.

"I'm sorry, guys, but I need to make a pit stop," Margo announced.

"Can't you wait 'til we get to the van?" Kenneth asked in an irritated voice.

"There isn't a bathroom in the van, so what good would that do? I drank a lot of juice."

"No problem. There's a large tree over there." Guillermo pointed. "We'll all wait here and look away to give you some privacy."

As they waited, Guillermo offered a short lesson about sloths and tapirs. Both creatures were big and helped to fertilize tree growth. Sloths were slow and tapirs were fast. He was discussing their habitat loss when a piercing scream rang out. The group whipped around as one and tentatively approached the large tree. Mateo held out his arm to keep the others back, but they could all see Margo holding up her shorts, her eyes bulging at an enormous snake inches away from her foot. It must have been eight feet long, and its tongue flicked ominously in and out.

"Nobody move," Mateo instructed. Guillermo slowly took his place, looking over Mateo's shoulder, and they conversed quietly in Spanish.

"Is that a boa constrictor?" Kelly asked.

"It sure as hell has the markings," Tia said.

"Do something!" Margo hissed. "It's going to bite me."

"It squeezes its prey," Mateo corrected. "A boa's bite is nonvenomous."

"I don't care," Margo said through clenched teeth. "Get it away from me!"

Guillermo took a few slow steps back, tore a thin branch off a tree, and stripped off its leaves. He returned and handed it to Mateo, who held it out in front of him like a cane. Mateo made some clicking noises to get the snake's attention, then tried to prod it away from Margo with the stick.

Instead of remaining still, Margo tried to run past the snake. It turned and instantly coiled its body around her ankle.

She whimpered. Everyone held their breath.

Iris carefully reached for her daypack and lifted out a pair of heavy binoculars. She edged closer to the snake, behind its line of vision.

Guillermo tried to stop her by whispering, "No. Stay back."

Iris darted forward and slammed the binoculars down on the snake's head.

The snake stopped moving, and the group froze, waiting to see if the creature was dead.

As the boa's body relaxed, Margo gingerly lifted her foot away from its limp coils and ran over to Kenneth, sobbing.

Tia called to Iris. "Holy shit. Some balls you've got, woman."

"Probably a stupid thing to do," Iris said, trying to scrape the gooey debris of the snake's head off her binoculars with a stick.

She looked up to see an expression of shock on Luc's face.

CHAPTER 23

On the ride back to the resort, Luc didn't say much, but Iris could feel disapproval emanating in her direction. All the other guests, especially Margo, had nothing but praise for Iris's dramatic and decisive action.

As Iris and Luc approached their casita, they could see the veranda lights had been turned on, highlighting a table set for their special dinner. Candles on the table were lit and exotic flowers spilled out from a vase.

Luc looked at her. "Did you arrange this?"

"I thought it could be nice for us to have a private dinner under the full moon."

He looked abashed. "Oh, good idea."

But lousy timing.

They went inside and Iris went to shower first. She leaned her head against the tile as tears slid silently down her cheeks and warm water washed over her. She had actually harbored a tiny hope that Luc might propose tonight. They'd been together for more than two years now and this first real vacation had been going so well. Until Luc's accident. And then Iris had done the one thing he had begged her not to do. She'd stuck her neck out, taking an unnecessary risk by trying to kill that snake. What was wrong with her?

When Iris emerged from the bathroom, wrapped in a towel, Luc was sitting on the bed looking at his phone. "Ellie texted us both another picture of Sheba." He handed it to her and walked across to the bathroom.

The sight of her sweet Basset hound playing with her stuffed chipmunk almost made her cry again. She could imagine the dog's faux-ferocious growls while tossing the toy in the air. Loving a canine was so uncomplicated.

Iris decided not to wear the elegant dress she had planned but threw on a simple sundress with a pashmina around her shoulders. Tonight could be a low-key affair, a chance to talk and clear the air. Maybe it would bring them closer. "Do you need any help in there?" she called out.

"No, I've got it," he replied.

There was a knock at the casita door and Iris opened it to find Sierra standing there holding a bottle of champagne. "You all were gone a long time at that waterfall. Do you still want dinner at seven?"

"Sure. I don't want to mess up Chef Vargas's timing. He's been so generous in making us this special meal. The table looks beautiful. Thank you for the champagne."

"I'll pop the cork and set it in the ice bucket outside. Carmen will bring your appetizers in ten minutes. It's a clear night, and the moon is perfectly full. Enjoy your meal."

Luc emerged from the bathroom and turned away from Iris as he dressed.

She went outside to look at the night sky. After her eyes adjusted, the stars seemed to pop. She could easily make out the face in the moon. It peered down at her with pity. She heard the door open and close behind her and felt Luc's hands resting on her shoulders.

He cleared his throat and said, "Thanks for arranging this dinner. I appreciate it."

They saw Carmen approaching and took their places at the table. She set down her tray on a stand and filled their flutes with champagne before placing down small plates with dollops of something white and gooey looking. "The amuse-bouches is a sea urchin soufflé. I'll be back shortly with your appetizers."

Mil gracias," Iris said.

Luc picked up the leaf on top of the sea urchin and tasted it. "Lemongrass. Did you design this menu, or did Santiago put it together?"

"We both did. I suggested the red snapper carpaccio for an appetizer and Chef Vargas created the amuse-bouches. The entrée is a surprise."

"I love surprises." He topped off their champagne glasses.

Carmen returned and replaced their plates with the appetizers. Luc took a bite and sighed deeply. His mood seemed to be improving.

It was time to rip off the band-aid. She took a long sip of champagne and looked into Luc's eyes. "I know you're unhappy that I put myself in danger this afternoon. We've talked about my getting involved in things that made you afraid for me. I don't know what came over me. Mateo did say the snake's bite was nonvenomous. But I was afraid that Margo, as ridiculous as she is, was going to have a stroke from fear."

She reached across the table and took Luc's hands in hers. "I'm sorry. I'll try harder. I don't want you to have to worry about me."

Luc looked down at their entwined hands. "Iris, my mother worried every morning when my father started his shift as a cop. Any time the doorbell would ring, she got scared. And then, on the day he was actually shot in the line of duty, no one rang the bell. He never came home. She had to call the station to start the search for him."

"I know, Luc. It must have been so hard for your family."

He looked at her beseechingly and slid his hand back to his lap. "I can't live like that. I don't want to live like that."

Their long, pained silence was broken a few minutes later by Carmen arriving with their entrées. Neither commented on the intricately presented bluefin tuna set before them, other than saying another "mil gracias" to Carmen.

Iris had lost her appetite. She'd heard many things in Luc's subdued voice: frustration, anger, and sadness. Was he to the point of breaking up with her? She had promised to try harder to stay out of danger. Did he not believe she could carry through on that? Then again, why should he believe her? She'd been kidnapped, shot at, and almost microwaved in the last year alone. And today, without blinking an eye, she'd leapt into action to kill a boa constrictor. Was this vacation a test and had she just failed it?

"You should try this tuna, Iris. The coconut, passion fruit, and pineapple marinade is very delicate."

Iris's mouth was bone-dry. It hurt to swallow. But she took a tiny bite and choked it down. So, this is what it had come down to? Discussing food as their means of communication? "Mmm. It *is* good." She imagined that they would be polite to each other for the rest of the trip and then, once back in Cambridge, they'd proceed to disentangle their lives. Her stomach tied in a knot. She loved Luc. She didn't want to break up.

Luc continued to make small talk during the meal—things he had learned about their fellow guests, which ingredients he guessed were in the dishes, future possible excursions Sierra had told him about. Iris made minimal responses. She felt broken. She wanted to sleep, wake up, and redo this day from scratch, and maybe get it right.

When Carmen came to collect the plates, she looked surprised at Iris's almost-untouched meal. "You didn't like it?"

Now, poor Santiago would feel insulted. "Oh, no. It's not that. I don't feel well. But please tell Chef Vargas that the bluefin was perfect." *Would this evening ever end?*

"I made up for Iris." Luc said, gesturing to his empty plate. "I'd love to get his recipe, especially for that fish marinade."

"I think you need something sweet to finish off the meal," Carmen pronounced, stacking the plates on her arm. She disappeared and returned a few minutes later, rolling a cart containing a kerosene stove and several cartons.

"What have you got there? A dessert flambé?" Luc asked.

"You'll see." Carmen drizzled dark rum over two split bananas in a skillet. She ignited the rum with a long lighter and swirled the pan. Flames leapt up and briefly illuminated the veranda. Luc looked on. She transferred the bananas and sauce into two bowls and added scoops of homemade ice cream. "Allí está!"

Luc clapped. "This is a feast, Carmen. You must give our compliments to Santiago."

Carmen tipped her head toward Iris. "It was your woman's idea. She planned the surprise."

Luc smiled at Iris. "It's a good surprise. Thank you."

Carmen rolled her cart away, and Iris tasted the Bananas Foster. It was ambrosial—warm and irresistible. Luckily, her stomach eased up and allowed her to eat all of it.

They finished the last bits. "Thank you for arranging that." Luc rested his napkin on the table. "I need some time to think. I'm going for a walk on the beach."

"Wait! Cal said it wasn't safe out there at night."

"I'll be fine."

CHAPTER 24

A giant hand seemed to press on Luc's chest as he left Iris and followed the path to the beach. He'd been a jerk after she'd gone to such trouble arranging the dinner, but he had meant what he'd said. Her behavior worried him. It reminded him of living with a father who faced danger every day, and it wasn't even Iris's job. Couldn't she control her impulse to step instinctively into scary situations in order to rescue people?

He stood in the sand, looking up at the stars in the deep velvet sky. They were bright enough but would have been spectacular if the full moon wasn't casting such a bright glow. Iris had timed their dinner to coincide with it. Why was a full moon supposed to be romantic? Was it a fertility thing, the fullness, or just the extra nighttime light?

Luc had enjoyed his fair share of romances. He'd even been married for a short time when he lived in Rome. But, with Iris, he finally felt like he was getting the relationship thing right. They were equally matched in dedication to work and enjoyed each other's company. Their life in the loft above his restaurant was good, la vida pura, in its own way. He didn't want that to end. How could he get Iris to change this one thing?

Luc scrambled over the rocks at the end of the cove to get to the long beach on the other side of the headland. When he reached it, he slipped off his sandals and set off walking in the heavy sand away from the resort. After a while, his calves began to ache. He sat down cross-legged, resting his heavy cast on his knee. Waves pounded the beach. Dark palm trees were silhouetted against the night sky. He tried to empty his mind, shut off his brain, and merely exist. The clicking of insects and chirping of frogs from the dense underbrush behind him formed a chorus of white noise. Mateo had called them poison dart frogs, toxic to touch and fatal to eat. Maybe he should offer them on the menu as frog's legs in a buttery garlic sauce when pain-in-the-ass customers dined at his restaurant. *Stop it, Luc. Turn your mind off and chill.*

After listening to the chorus of nature sounds with his eyes closed, the whining of a motor interrupted his serenity. Luc opened his eyes and searched the faint ocean horizon but saw nothing. After a few moments, the engine noise cut out. Luc thought he saw a light flash twice. Or was it a reflection on the waves? No, it looked like it came from a boat travelling with its running lights turned off. Was it a signal directed at someone on the shore?

He glanced down the beach and caught a slight movement breaking out from the underbrush. He crouched and backed up slowly to blend in with the darkness of the trees, finding a baseball cap from his pocket to cover his blond hair. A few moments later, two bursts of light from the far end of the beach were directed back toward the boat. Luc felt a rising sense of alarm.

Was there some innocent reason for this interaction? He tried to think of one. It was the lack of running lights that had him most concerned. Clearly, no one was meant to know they were there or see what was about to happen.

The motor started up again and got steadily louder. Luc could make out a small dark shape moving swiftly toward the shore. His heart pounded loudly as the long, narrow hull of a powerful cigarette boat slowed and circled to a stop barely twenty yards away. A shadowy figure came along the sand, dragging something toward the boat. He lifted what looked like a crate, hunching over as he entered the surf. Luc could make out two people on the boat leaning down to receive the cargo. As soon as the crate was whisked out of sight, the boat started up again, backed away, and sped off. The figure on the beach disappeared into the thicket of trees.

Luc didn't dare move. What the hell was he supposed to do now?

By the time Luc crept back to the cottage, Iris was asleep. He wanted to tell her what he'd seen at the beach, but after giving her such a hard time about courting danger, he couldn't let her see him doing the same thing.

He got undressed and slipped into bed, trying not to wake her. As he tried to fall asleep, his mind kept rehashing the night's strange activities. What was inside that crate? Drugs, guns ... a body? Cal had warned the guests that it wasn't safe to go out to the beach at night. Why was that? Was Cal part of what was going on? What else could he be referring to other than possible smuggling? Dangerous animals creeping out from the jungle?

This was crazy. It was not his problem to figure out. For all he knew, the proper authorities were already monitoring this operation and were ready to jump in and make arrests if that was needed. He hoped the resort wasn't involved. Cal and Sierra seemed like good people. They were trying to help the villagers by providing a major source of jobs, plus funding the orphanage and promoting local artists.

He would put this out of his mind and focus on enjoying the rest of their vacation.

CHAPTER 25

When Luc woke up the next morning, he blinked across the room and saw that Iris was already up, dressed, and brushing her hair. Her eyes looked puffy.

She turned from the mirror. "I wasn't sure if I should wake you since you must have gotten in pretty late."

He sat up in bed. "About last night. I'm sorry I was in such a bad mood. You tried to make it a special evening and I ruined it." He walked over to her and leaned his head against hers, pressing his lips lightly next to her ear. "I want us to be together. We'll figure out how to deal with my stressing out about you. It's a hot-button issue, but we can work out some kind of solution."

Her head was now buried in his chest, so he couldn't gauge her reaction. When she looked up a moment later, there were tears in her eyes.

"I thought you were breaking up with me."

He shook his head. "I can't imagine living without you." He leaned down to kiss her.

A little while later, they walked together into the dining pavilion for breakfast, holding hands.

"Look at those two lovebirds," Margo called out from her table. "I think *we* need to have a romantic dinner at *our* casita, Kenneth."

After breakfast, Luc accompanied Iris to her surfing lesson so he could try to capture a video of her best rides. But first, he wanted to take a stroll. Giving Iris a thumbs-up for luck, he headed for the headland. He glanced around to make sure that no one was watching him before clambering over the rocks to the deserted beach beyond. After twenty minutes of walking, he figured he was standing close to where the mystery man had loaded the cigarette boat.

Was there any sign of last night's activities? He walked toward the water to look for drag marks or footprints. He searched for cigarette butts or other telltale debris in the sand. But either the tide had washed away all traces, the phantom figures had been careful, or he'd hallucinated the whole thing.

By midafternoon, Luc had convinced himself he needed to tell Iris about the cigarette boat. Full transparency. That's what he wanted from her, so that's what he should provide.

Lying in the hammock on the veranda with his eyes closed, he heard Iris's footsteps returning from the yoga class. He attempted to get up out of the hammock.

"Wow. You should try that class," she said. "I'm sure Sierra could adapt the poses to avoid stress on your poor arm." She came over to help him stand and to join her on the loveseat.

"Maybe. I do need to get more exercise."

Iris slid the elastic off her ponytail and shook down her hair. "What have you been up to while I've been out there standing on my head?"

"Ah..." He hesitated, then blurted out, "I may have seen something being smuggled onto a boat last night."

"Where? When?" Iris pulled back from him, staring.

"After dinner, when I was walking along the beach beyond the cove. I saw some flashes of light from a boat with no running lights on. There were a few return flashes from someone on the shore. Then, a man dragged a crate out of the jungle onto the beach. The boat came in close, and two men heaved the crate onboard before the boat sped off. It was one of those fast cigarette boats."

"The kind that drug smugglers use?"

"Yeah."

"My God, Luc. Did any of them see you?"

"No, I was in the dark, back in the underbrush."

"Why didn't you tell me? If they'd seen you, they might have shot you or drowned you in the surf!"

"I was going to, but you were asleep when I got back. Then, this morning, I wondered if the whole thing was just in my imagination."

"Sounds way too detailed for a hallucination. Wait! Do you think the men and the boat had anything to do with the missing relics?"

"More likely they were smuggling drugs, or maybe guns headed to Nicaragua. Do you think we should tell anyone?"

"You mean Cal and Sierra? No! They're the ones who warned us to stay off the beach at night. They could be mixed up in this." Iris's eyes found his. "You do realize what's happening, don't you?"

He cocked his head quizzically. "What do you mean?"

"Despite a warning, *you* went out on the beach at night and could have gotten yourself killed! Now, we're sitting here trying to piece together what these night-time operators were doing and wondering if it relates to robberies we learned about. This is exactly the way *I've* gotten sucked into hairy situations that have caused you so much anxiety."

"Oof." Luc's shoulders slumped. "You're right. Let's back off. It's terrible someone stole these artifacts, and there might be some fishy things happening on the beach at night, but I don't have any proof about what might have been in that crate. And I certainly don't want those guys to know that I was spying on them."

"Agreed."

CHAPTER 26

Iris changed into a silk jumpsuit for dinner as she surveyed Luc behind her in the mirror. He was struggling to get a long-sleeved shirt over his cast. A shock of blond hair hung over one eye. She still felt unmoored by his statement the night before that he couldn't keep on living the way they had been. It hadn't occurred to her that their relationship was in trouble. Now, no matter how much she tried to believe things were back to normal, it felt like something had broken. Would it make any difference in Luc's thinking now that the tables had turned, and he'd seen how easy it was to fall down that rabbit hole?

"Here, let me help with that," she offered.

"Thanks. I'm sick of wearing short-sleeved shirts. They make me look like a golfer."

She fastened his buttons, leaving his left wrist rolled up. "There." She glanced at her watch. "We should go. Oh, I forgot to mention, after yoga class I invited Lisa and Kelly to join us for dinner. That okay with you?"

"Sure. I never got a chance to ask them how they started a vineyard from scratch."

That evening, salsa music played in the background as happy cocktail hour chatter filled the pavilion. Iris and Luc headed for the bar, nodding and smiling at the other guests as they passed.

Iris ordered herself a Bombay Sapphire Martini, feeling the need for a serious drink to jump-start her spirits. They stood at the bar while Luc had Sammy concoct some kind of complicated fruit and rum drink.

The salsa music segued into something more mellow, and the guests moved toward their dinner tables. Iris waved to Lisa, and the two couples converged on a table set up for four.

Lisa sat next to Luc. "How's the arm?" she asked.

"It's stopped hurting, mainly. But it's still awkward to sleep with a cast, so I'm pretty tired."

"That should get better soon."

"Are you keeping busy during the day?" Kelly asked him after giving her drink order to the server. Kelly and Lisa had chosen cocktails instead of wine. Maybe they needed a sabbatical from their profession.

"I've basically been reading and exercising in the pool." Luc squeezed an orange slice into his cocktail. "I noticed you jogging on the beach before breakfast this morning. Do you run past the headland to the next beach over?"

"Yes. The far beach extends another mile or so," Kelly answered. "I like to get in some decent cardio. You a runner?"

"At home, I'm usually dealing with food venders in the morning, then prepping all afternoon for the dinner crowd. I don't have much time for exercise," he said. "But maybe I should start running while I'm here."

Iris noticed Kelly's eyes sweep appraisingly over Luc's toned body.

"Speaking of the beach," Iris said, diverting Kelly's attention, "What's the deal with us keeping away from it at night? Do you know the reason for that?"

"Cal told us a jaguar lives in the jungle over by the far beach," Lisa said.

Iris swallowed. "Seriously?"

Lisa continued, "It's not a problem during the day. Cal said it only comes out to hunt at night."

Iris gently kicked Luc's shin under the table.

Luc had trouble sleeping that night. How could he have been so nonchalant about Cal's warning? The possibility of a wild beast ripping him apart for its dinner made him feel nauseous. He'd already broken his arm on this vacation. Then the cigarette boat affair and the jaguar. Exposure to life-and-death situations hadn't been listed as a feature in that magazine article raving about the Guaria Morada Resort.

CHAPTER 27

In the dim light of the early morning, Iris slept soundly beside him. Had he somehow put her in danger by bringing her here? As Luc stared up at the ceiling, the irony of the situation was loud and clear.

After breakfast, he walked with Iris to the beach, wishing the whole time that he could be out in the waves, too. On the way back to the casita, he noticed Margo wasn't stationed on her usual chaise lounge. The coast was clear. He hurried back to the room and struggled, one-handed, into his swimming trunks.

There was still no sight of her by the time Luc shoved his cast into its protective cover and eased himself down the steps into the shallow end of the pool. He covered six laps fast-walking across its width before Margo made her appearance. She was decked out in a huge sunhat, sunglasses with prominent gold logos on the sides, and a bikini that was asking for a wardrobe malfunction. She lowered herself into a chaise facing the beach.

"Hi, handsome. It's just us again."

"Trying to get some exercise..." Luc winced as soon as the words were out of his mouth, anticipating some innuendo about a better way to exert himself, but she remained silent.

Margo fanned out her stack of magazines on a low table, along with a glass of clear liquid with some ice and a sprig of mint. A mojito, no doubt. Was she looped already?

Luc continued his laps until he'd counted fifty, twisted back and forth to stretch, and climbed out of the pool.

Margo waved him over to the chaise next to hers, which she'd covered with a towel.

He figured he'd stay for a short while before escaping back to the casita. Where was the new pool guy? He'd feel safer with a chaperone.

Margo made a circle in the air with her sunglasses. "I had Sammy bring you some ice water." She tipped her head toward the second glass on the table between them. Her words sounded slightly slurred. Luc hadn't noticed the bartender coming and going. Margo probably had him on timed visits for refills.

Luc toweled himself off, trying not to notice Margo watching him intently. But when he did hazard a look up, she was staring at some point over his shoulder. She frowned and shook her head fractionally. He glanced around in time to see Mateo on the path, quickly retreating toward the beach. What was that all about? Perhaps a rendezvous that Margo didn't want Luc to know about?

She studied him through half-lidded eyes. "Nice swim?"

"Refreshing. Are you a swimmer?"

"Was on the varsity swim team at Texas A&M. Go Aggies!"

Luc laughed. He lay back in his chaise and grabbed the glass of water. As he took a sip, he noticed green leaves floating on the surface. The other glass had no mint. He had mistakenly drunk from Margo's glass. She was loading up on ice water.

CHAPTER 28

Iris thought about the game of musical chairs. Every seat tonight was already taken, except for the two empty ones at Margo and Kenneth's table for four.

Margo was standing up waving at them, as if they could miss her in that gold, sequined dress which reflected all the light in the room.

"We arranged for you to eat with us tonight!" Margo said. Kenneth was already seated and studying the menu. "We haven't had much chance to chat," Margo said.

Iris and Luc pasted on their best smiles and took the two unoccupied seats, Luc across from Margo and Iris facing the unwelcoming Kenneth.

"You two are quite the dancers," Luc said as he shook out his napkin and placed it on his lap.

"We know how to have a good time." Kenneth grabbed Margo's hand. "Don't we, Sugar?"

Margo ignored her boyfriend, her attention fully centered on Luc. "You're not so bad yourself at shaking that booty."

This was going to be a long dinner. Then again, it might be an opportunity for Iris to figure out what Kenneth's deal was.

When their server appeared, Kenneth asked the small group, "Another cocktail? Glass of wine?" Leaving no time for consultation,

Margo ordered champagne for the table, and they added their appetizer orders.

Iris closed her menu. "Kenneth, you're from Houston, right? What do you do there?" Around Boston, it was gauche to ask people what they did for a living, but she was pretty sure different rules existed in other parts of the country.

"I trade cattle futures. Know anything about it?"

"Can't say that I do." *Or want to.* "You must explain it to me sometime."

"And just what do *you* do?" Kenneth asked Iris.

"I'm an architect. I'm designing a museum at the moment."

"Make any money at it?" He asked.

"I do okay," Iris said. *We are really not in New England anymore.* "How about you, Margo? Didn't I hear that you also have a business in Houston?"

Margo leaned toward Iris and Luc until her ample bosom was nearly flattened out on the table. "I have a small boutique in the River Oaks District. We sell contemporary art, crafts, and jewelry, that sort of thing."

"Do you carry pottery?" Iris asked. "We visited a pottery studio in a nearby village on Monday and I bought some beautiful bowls."

"I have a source in Mexico that manufactures all my pottery."

"But maybe we should go check out the local place," Kenneth suggested. "It can't hurt to look at other vendors. I'll bet the trade prices down here are pretty cheap."

"We don't have a car, Kenny." Margo turned back to speak directly to Luc, as if Iris and *Kenny* weren't there. "How did you get to the village?"

"Mateo let us ride along with him on Monday, and we tagged along with Lisa and Kelly on Wednesday," Luc said.

Margo smirked. "You get around."

Why did everything the woman said sound like a tacky sexual innuendo? Iris was one glass of wine away from calling her out on it.

Instead, to direct the conversation away from Luc, Iris told Margo and Kenneth what she knew about the theft of the Crying Crocodile and its three companion pieces.

When she finished the story, Kenneth shook his head in disbelief. "That's terrible. Who would do such a thing?"

Margo's eyes lit up. "It's awful, of course. But how big did you say that emerald was?"

CHAPTER 29

The next morning, after dropping Iris off at her surf class, Luc scrambled over the rocky promontory to the outer beach, remembering Kelly's assertion that jaguars slept during the day. He fished his sling out of his daypack and slipped it around his cast to support his arm. The shoreline down as far as he could see showed no evidence of any wild animals, and the heat wasn't too oppressive yet.

Luc did a few stretches, then started jogging along the shore. The tide must have gone out recently because the sand near the water's edge was packed hard, and he could pick up some speed. His balance was a little wonky because of the cast, but it felt so good to be moving that he soon accelerated into a full-out run. He kept up that pace for fifteen minutes, travelling far down the long beach, when suddenly, he felt a sharp tightening in his calf. His muscle spasmed in a painful cramp.

Luc collapsed onto the sand, desperately trying to stretch out his leg, and fumbled in his pack for some water. It spilled out the sides of his mouth as he guzzled half the bottle. He tried to take deep breaths, but stabs of pain kept flaring up. *So much for moderation, Cormier!*

He'd gotten a nasty charley horse the previous year while playing Ultimate Frisbee on the Cambridge Common with his Sunday-afternoon league. His friend Declan had showed him how to flex his toes up and back toward his knee. He tried it now, pulling hard on the toes. Gradually, the pain receded.

Luc took long, deep breaths while sitting cross-legged in the sand. He got a tiny green banana out of his pack and ate it absently as he looked out to sea. A flock of screaming gulls swooped down to investigate the peel, but quickly lost interest after Luc stashed it away.

There were several boats out in the distance, none moving very quickly. He found Tia's borrowed binoculars in his bag and focused them on the boats. One looked like a dilapidated fishing boat, anchored in place. Behind it, near the horizon, he could make out a huge cruise ship. Finally, a single-mast sailboat floated slowly along, the wind failing to fill its sail. There were no hot-rod cigarette boats in sight.

Luc directed the binoculars toward the jungle. Could he catch a glimpse of that jaguar? Did he really want to? The sand abruptly changed to dirt and moss. The undergrowth was dense, with long tree branches stretching out and touching the ground. Looking closely at the green wall of the rain forest, Luc detected a slight opening in the trees.

He stood slowly, tentatively putting weight on his leg. With the daypack returned to his back, Luc crossed the twenty-foot expanse of sand, reminding himself that a large predatory creature lived in this jungle, and might well be watching him. As he approached the edge of the vegetation, the slapping sound of the ocean's waves gave way to the chittering of insects, birds, and other small animals. Now he could see the shadowed opening more clearly. There was a narrow dirt path, and it led straight back into the jungle. What was this land used for? Where did the path go?

Luc adjusted the focus of the binoculars and aimed them along the path. He took a few steps into the underbrush. There was something large and tan, set about thirty feet in. He moved off to the side to get a better view. It looked like a straw structure. He eased to the other side. Maybe a hut. He was about to take a few steps closer when he glanced down and noticed a distinct mark in the dirt. The imprint of a sneaker. He looked closer. It looked like it belonged to a man's shoe. The footprints continued in the direction of the hut. Who would dare venture into the jungle where a jaguar was said to live?

The loud crack of a breaking branch splintered the air. Luc froze, instantly alert. It came from the brush nearby. His nerve endings bristled. He turned and raced back toward the resort.

CHAPTER 30

When Luc arrived back at the resort cove, his heart rate had slowed to normal, but he was still freaked out. All the students were in the water, involved in various stages of riding waves, except Tia. She lay on her back on a towel in the sand, sunglasses on.

Luc pulled a towel out of his pack and put the cover on his cast. "Okay if I join you?"

"I'm just taking a break," she said, not looking over.

"No judgment," Luc lowered himself onto the towel.

They lay side by side in companionable silence for several minutes before Tia turned and asked, "Is there a way men prefer for women to break up with them?"

"Hmm. Trouble in Paradise?"

"Too much time together." Tia lifted herself onto her elbows, dropping her sunglasses down her nose. "We were fine in L.A. when Eric was working most of the time. But now I've had plenty of chance to see what an asshole he is."

Luc couldn't disagree with her assessment. He did a speed-catalog of his own past break-ups. "Wait until you're back home, then give him the 'I need some space' line. He'll get swept up with the restaurant again, and you can ease your way out."

"Yeah, I was gravitating toward that approach." She sat up and looked out to sea. "Iris has made a lot of progress staying up on the board."

Luc shaded his eyes to pick out Iris riding a large wave in to shore. She did look good. He thought he could even see her fierce look of concentration. He was proud of her and wished they could be doing this together.

"Bummer about your arm," Tia said. "How have you been keeping busy?"

"I finished the three books I brought, I've been exercising in the pool, and we've been taking some excursions into town."

"See anything interesting?"

"We visited a pottery studio and a small museum on Monday. Iris and I went back on Wednesday with Kelly and Lisa to show them this cool ancient artifact, but thieves had stolen it overnight, and murdered the guard!"

"Whaaat? A robbery and murder happened around here this week?"

Before he knew it, Luc was telling Tia the whole story. He told her about Julio's missing cousin, the cigarette boat, and even about the hut in the jungle inhabited by a jaguar.

"Holy shit. How did I miss all this drama? This is better than a true crime podcast!" Tia said. "I was so bored, but now we have a real-life mystery to solve. And it's happening now! Where do we start?"

Luc groaned and turned face-down on his towel. Why did everyone have a case of detective fever?

CHAPTER 31

This time, Iris rode the wave to shore in a purely reactive state. She didn't think about the movements her body needed to execute. It all flowed.

As she splashed back through the foamy water to the beach, she noticed Luc and Tia sitting together. She dropped her board on the sand and jogged over to them. "What are you two up to, lounging about?"

Luc rolled over toward Iris and smiled up at her. "It's the Surf Queen."

"Your boyfriend was giving me advice on my love life," Tia said.

It took a beat before Iris responded. "Uh, okay. Was it good advice?"

"Since it matched what I was planning to do anyway, I think it was brilliant." Tia rose and brushed sand off her hands. Guillermo was dragging surfboards toward the beach hut. "Looks like class is over. I'm going to take a shower before lunch. See you there." She waved as she headed off toward her casita.

Iris cocked an eyebrow at Luc. "So, you're a relationship expert now? How interesting."

"Only compared to Eric." He stood up, shook out his towel, and stuffed it in his pack. "It's a low bar. She wants to break up with him."

Iris sighed. "As if we don't have enough drama going on around this place."

On entering the pavilion for lunch, Iris quickly gravitated toward a small table set up for two and pulled Luc toward it. She wasn't in the mood to be social. On their way across the room, she and Luc passed Tia talking excitedly with Lisa and Kelly. Iris heard Tia say something about a hut, but she didn't hear the context.

"I hope this won't be awkward," Iris said, taking her seat. "Us knowing that Tia wants to ditch Eric before he's aware of it."

"I wish she hadn't told me," Luc said. "Maybe we'll get lucky, and won't have much contact with him over this last week."

Today's lunch was a buffet. Iris and Luc got up to examine today's tempting choices when Sierra intercepted them.

"Luc," Sierra said. "I've arranged with Chef Vargas for you and Eric to join him in the kitchen at five tonight. He can show you around the vegetable garden, and then he'll walk you through the preparation for tonight's dinner. Would you enjoy that?"

"That sounds great, Sierra. Thanks."

After she retreated to her own table, Luc grimaced. "So much for not crossing paths with Eric."

Once everyone had finished eating and was lingering over cups of coffee or tea, Cal strode over to the bar area to connect the videos he'd taken of the morning's surf session to a large TV monitor. But before he could dim the lights, two official-looking men bustled into the pavilion, scanned the room, and approached Cal. The one wearing a suit leaned in and spoke to him in a low voice. Both he and his companion produced badges, which Cal examined carefully.

By now, everyone in the room was silent and trying to listen to their conversation. Sierra hurried over, and Cal whispered something in her ear. She nodded, pulled out a phone from her pants pocket, and scurried out the front door.

Cal frowned and his eyes darted over to Iris and Luc. She gripped Luc's hand and he squeezed it back. *Were they in trouble? For what?*

The three men headed over to their table.

"What did you guys do?" Eric called out. "Steal a trinket from a souvenir stall?" Tia shushed him as Luc glared at Eric.

Cal leaned down and said to them, "Lieutenant Alvarez and Officer Diaz would like to speak with you privately about your trip to the Santa Elena Museum the other day. Why don't we all go to my office?"

In the silence that followed, Iris sensed many sets of eyes following their procession out of the room.

CHAPTER 32

Is this job cursed? First, my idiot helpers shoot the guard. Then the guard's cousin mysteriously disappears, and I have no way of knowing what she might have seen or heard. Let's hope this Ana person is too scared to show back up.

And that damn Luc Cormier happening to witness the smugglers picking up the last urn? And him finding the hut? Lucky for me Tia is such a gossip, and I have sharp ears. What are the odds the guy would be on that stretch of beach at midnight on that exact night? Is he undercover? I need to dig into his background. Maybe the broken arm was a faked accident to give him free time to snoop around in the mornings while everyone else is surfing.

The only good news is that the complete animal quartet with all their jewels made it out of the country. The buyer will be pleased. Three of them are already in the U.S. and the fourth is travelling along the expected route up through Mexico.

I almost lost my cool when the police showed up and marched off Luc and Iris. I need to find out what that was about. If I'm lucky, the cops suspect them. Maybe I can encourage that thought.

CHAPTER 33

Iris had wondered about the empty casita closest to the pavilion. As Cal unlocked the door, she saw quickly that it was the resort's management office.

Instead of bedroom furniture, the space was laid out with a large desk, cabinets, a sofa, and chairs. Since the air conditioning hadn't been turned on, the room felt warm and muggy. Cal flipped a switch inside the door and the whirring sound of a fan started up.

They all stood there awkwardly while the officers showed their badges to Iris and Luc and introduced themselves.

"These men are from the O.I.J., which is the investigative branch of the Costa Rican police," Cal explained. "Sierra has gone to call our local lawyer. If you'd feel more comfortable, you can wait until he arrives before you answer any questions. I can stay to explain how things work here, or go, as you wish."

Iris looked over at Luc, who shrugged. "Why don't you stay, Cal." Luc said.

"We have nothing to hide," Iris said to Lieutenant Alvarez, a serious-looking man with a full black beard.

They sat down, Iris and Luc on the sofa, the two officers in armchairs, and Cal behind the desk.

"What can we help you with?" Iris asked, leaning gently back, trying to look relaxed.

Alvarez pressed the record button on his phone. "We learned that on Monday afternoon, the thirtieth of December, you both visited the Museum at Santa Elena at around three o'clock and saw the jade urn of the Crying Crocodile. Is that correct?"

Iris and Luc nodded.

"Please make a verbal response for the record," the lieutenant instructed.

"Yes," Luc and Iris repeated simultaneously.

"The museum guard said that you expressed a lot of interest in the piece."

Oh, swell. Were they accusing her and Luc of the theft? Had they been the last ones to see it? "It was the centerpiece of the exhibit. We thought it was interesting," Iris said. "The guard was there when we left."

"You are an architect, Señora Reid. Is that correct?"

Iris nodded, then remembered to respond out loud, "Yes." Did her profession make her appear more likely to covet an artifact?

"And you are a cook, Señor Cormier?" Alvarez asked Luc.

"A chef and owner of a restaurant," Luc said, sounding irritated at the demotion.

"When did you both enter the country?"

"Last Saturday, December the twenty-eighth," Luc answered.

"Where were you both on New Year's Eve?"

"We were here at the resort's party with everybody else," Iris replied. "We left the party around ten because we were tired. Luc had broken his arm that morning and was on strong medication." Iris suddenly remembered the stern advice of her attorney brother, Sterling, to briefly answer questions from the police without elaborating.

The police officer's questions continued, focusing on every detail of their afternoon and evening including the names of witnesses who could confirm their movements. But it was their last question that surprised Iris the most.

"How well did you know the museum's night watchman, Julio Sanchez? I understand he worked at the resort."

. . .

"I'd seen him around once or twice," Luc said.

Iris wondered if she should wait for the resort's attorney before answering. But she had done nothing wrong. "As a favor to Sierra, I sketched up the design of some guards to keep the monkeys off the casita roofs, and Julio was installing them. We talked a little then," Iris said.

"When was this?" Alvarez asked.

Iris hesitated. "Before we went to the New Year's Eve dinner."

"Which you and Mr. Cormier left early, at ten p.m."

CHAPTER 34

Iris dreaded the thought that she might need to call Sterling to extract her from another mess. Did her slight connection to the stolen artifact and to Julio make her a suspect, or was Lieutenant Alvarez fishing?

Alvarez and Diaz were winding up the interview when someone knocked on the door and a man in Bermuda shorts entered. He was shaped like a wine barrel on toothpick legs. Cal strode across the room to shake hands. "Mark, thanks for coming on short notice."

Cal made formal introductions all around, and Lieutenant Alvarez explained to Mark Harris that he was investigating Wednesday night's robbery and murder at the Santa Elena Museum.

Cal said, "These officers wanted to speak to our guests, and I thought we should err on the safe side and have you present."

"Always a good idea," Mark agreed. "Although we'd have to make sure there were no conflicts with the resort's interests." He peered over his horn-rimmed glasses at Iris and Luc, seeming to size them up.

"As it turns out, Iris and Luc have already filled them in on the little they know," Cal continued, "so I may have raised a false alarm."

"Why don't you read me in on the details," the attorney said, and they all sat down to go over Iris and Luc's testimony again. Over the course of the conversation, Harris pointed out that clearly the urn was still in its case when Iris and Luc left the museum, and that their connection to Julio was insubstantial.

Alvarez and Diaz stood up and thanked everyone for their time. Cal walked the officers out while Harris remained in the room. His eyes, behind their thick glasses, looked expectant. "So, what aren't you telling me?"

"Nothing," Luc protested. "We read in the Tica Times about thieves stealing all four important artifacts, but we had nothing to do with it. And we certainly didn't murder anyone. We came to Costa Rica to learn to surf!"

Harris studied them. "The O.I.J. will delve into your backgrounds. Have you had any suspicious dealings in the past with crimes?"

Luc looked over at Iris. "I'd better let Iris answer that one."

Iris was pretty sure she had portrayed her past involvement with law enforcement cases in the best possible light to Mark Harris, Esquire. But his parting words were, "We'll have to wait and see what the O.I.J. does next." That didn't sound like he thought Iris and Luc's involvement had been ruled out.

Now, half an hour later, she sat on the veranda with Luc, pretending to read her book while her mind kept wandering. The irony was that this time she hadn't actively done anything to get involved in a case. They had visited a museum while on vacation. What could be more innocent than that? If anything, Luc had showed more curiosity about the robberies than her, searching online for articles about the "Animal Quartet," the media's new term for the missing artifacts. He had even found an article about the thefts on NYT.com, so the news had spread.

Luc looked over from the hammock, his iPad resting on his stomach. "Do you think Mark Harris' legal fees are part of our Guaria Morada all-inclusive package?"

Iris gave him a sardonic look. "Maybe if it turns out to be a one-off meeting since the resort called him in. But if we need longer-term representation, we may have to fly Sterling down here."

Luc groaned. "Oh, come on. The O.I.J. can't railroad us! We haven't done anything wrong. We weren't even in the country for the first three thefts."

"I feel like there's something we're missing here. Some information that Alvarez or his partner aren't telling us."

"Like what?"

Iris scratched a mosquito bite on her leg. "Something that connects the crime to this resort beyond the fact that Julio worked here."

Iris wasn't aware of Kelly walking up behind her until she heard the young woman's voice. "Are you trying to figure out the mystery without us? Let us help." She and Lisa made themselves comfortable on the veranda chairs.

"Why did those official-looking guys drag you off? You didn't steal the Crying Crocodile, did you?"

"Kelly!" her mother exclaimed. "Of course they didn't. They don't fit the profile."

"What profile?" Luc rolled out of the hammock and joined them at a seat around the table.

"We contacted Sara Jane McClinnock, the podcaster for *Real Crimes in Real Time*," Lisa said. "She and her followers have solved dozens of cases. We told her everything we know about this crime so far and Sara Jane actually texted us back! She's going to feature our crime on her show!"

Iris shuddered. A few months earlier, a podcaster had misquoted her on air and given her museum project a nasty nickname. Her client was not happy.

Kelly went on. "Sara Jane has this psychiatrist listener who volunteers to provide profiles for her various cases. Sometimes they're eerily accurate."

Luc asked, "Are shrinks allowed to free-lance like that? It doesn't sound very professional."

Iris rolled her eyes. "So, what was his profile for this thief?"

Kelly read the text from her phone, "Dr. Fred gives a bunch of disclaimers first, then says it's likely to be a white man, between fifty and sixty, from the U.S. or Europe. He's organized; he plans. But then he often acts on impulse. The suspect would have two or three younger men working for him, with one having the advanced hacking skills to disconnect the museum security systems. Also, this probably wouldn't be his first time stealing a collection from a minimally guarded museum or gallery, so the police should look for similar crimes."

"Well, that lets Iris and I off the suspects list," Luc said. "What a relief!"

"Dr. Fred?" Iris said dubiously.

"He doesn't want to use his last name," Kelly explained.

"I wonder why," Iris muttered. "Luc and I were wondering if the O.I.J., which is the investigative branch of the police here, might have some evidence linking this resort to the crime. For one thing, Julio, the guy who worked at the pool here, was moonlighting as the museum's night watchman. He was killed during the robbery."

"That nice young man with the parrot tattoo?" Lisa asked, looking over at her daughter. "That's terrible."

"That is sad. We have to tell this to Sara Jane. She needs to know all the facts," Kelly said. "Maybe she can dig into any connections between the crime and the resort."

"Is involving a podcaster a good idea?" Iris asked. "Sometimes the podcast followers misidentify the criminal and end up harassing innocent people. If we point them toward this resort, they could decide that any of us is guilty."

"But if they listen to Dr. Fred," Lisa said, "the only ones who fit his profile are Kenneth or Cal."

CHAPTER 35

The four of them discussed what they knew about Kenneth and Cal, but it wasn't much. Certainly nothing incriminating.

Iris felt relieved when Kelly and Lisa finally got up and left the veranda. She tried to organize her thoughts while, across the table, Luc stared intently at his iPad.

"I hate podcasters," Iris muttered. "This is turning into a nightmare."

"I did a search on her. This Sara Jane person has over two thousand rabid listeners who all see themselves as Nancy Drew. They're going to be raking over the lives of everyone even marginally involved, including all of us guests and the staff at the resort."

"Oh, God. Can we convince Kelly and Lisa to call off the dogs?"

"Too late," Luc said. "Once this type of internet fan is unleashed, there's no turning back. Sara Jane has already downloaded her first chapter, laying out the basics of the Animal Quartet robberies."

"But when they run Google searches on everybody, *we* should look innocent enough, right?"

"I just checked," Luc said. "*I* look fine."

"Meaning what?"

"Remember when you got arrested for that bank robbery?"

"*Falsely* arrested."

"The article about the arrest shows up a full browser page before *The Boston Globe's* retraction."

"Damn. The O.I.J. is probably going to see that."

"And then there's a mention of you giving an alibi for that Dutch pedophile at Harvard."

"But the alibi was accurate."

"Technically. You won't get the sympathy vote for that, though."

Iris groaned. "What else?"

Luc scrolled down further. "The dead bodies in your museum project…the skeleton in the chimney at the art studio…"

Iris held up her hand. "Okay, okay. I've been involved with murder cases before. But I don't fit Dr. Fred's profile, and this case is primarily about robberies, right? Poor Julio must have been in the thief's way."

"Even so, you should call Elvis in Cambridge and have him clean up your search history."

"I'll send him an email now. But this Sara Jane character may have already checked me out."

Iris composed some urgent instructions to her tech consultant, reread her email, and sent it to Elvis. But she continued to worry about the podcaster pinning a target on her back. Hopefully, the O.I.J. would discover the identity of the actual thief soon.

She glanced at her watch. Almost time to get ready for yoga. Iris needed to quiet her mind and relax with some difficult, extended stretches. Maybe a headstand would empty her mind of anxiety. She needed to stop visualizing Julio's gentle eyes and hearing him talk about his dream to go to architecture school. Then there was the other conversation she'd overheard a few days earlier outside the massage hut between Julio and a friend. What had the friend been saying was too dangerous? Moonlighting as a night watchman to protect the remaining artifact? And who was this friend who was warning him?

CHAPTER 36

Luc gave five seconds of thought to whether he should change out of his low-slung sweatpants and T-shirt after Yoga class. He was a little sweaty, but Eric and Chef Vargas wouldn't care. He hurried through the pavilion and pushed open the door to the kitchen.

Eric was already there, predictably, the weenie. He was wearing a sweaty muscle shirt and terrycloth shorts.

"Hi, Chef Vargas, Eric. Am I late?" Luc asked.

"Please, call me Santiago. We're all chefs here. And no, you're right on time." Santiago was maybe forty, a few years older than Luc. He had a deep, resonant voice and a confident manner.

Eric mouthed behind Santiago's back, "You're late."

"You been working out?" Luc asked him in a low voice.

"Pumping iron in the gym. You lift?"

"Yeah, cartons of meat and canned food. I didn't know there was a gym here."

"It's in a palapa next to the last casita."

Luc had noticed that the kitchen was small and simple compared to his gleaming, stainless-steel restaurant kitchen back in Cambridge. Which made the complex meals Santiago had produced here even more impressive. Two young women were sitting at a table by a window, silently cutting up sweet chili peppers next to a bowl of soaking beans.

Santiago handed big market baskets to Luc and Eric. "I thought we'd start out back." He led them outside to where a flourishing garden was surrounded by reed fencing. Several fruit trees shaded the back corner, and a raised bed with herbs ran along the kitchen wall. The variety of what he saw impressed Luc. Not the heartier salad options you could grow in New England, but tropical things he barely recognized like chayote, yuca and dragon fruit. He headed over to the trees and peered at a bright red ball covered in green hair clinging to a branch. "This fruit is crazy. Straight out of Dr. Seuss."

"That's a Mamón Chino, but it won't be ripe until next summer." Santiago tipped his head. "It tastes like a fruity gummy bear, but better than that. Hard to explain. I use it to flavor flan."

"It's like a rambutan. We have them in California." Eric tore off a small piece of cilantro and lifted it to his nose to smell. "This garden is impressive. L.A. has a decent growing season, but here you can grow the more exotic things. I'd love to concoct some recipes using this stuff."

As they followed the path around the garden, Santiago picked or pulled up various greens and vegetables and loaded them into Eric and Luc's baskets. "We're offering sea bream, pork Casado and a vegetable tamale for entrees tonight. And I thought I'd show you how I make the sea urchin appetizer that Luc tasted on Thursday night."

Thirty minutes later, Luc had managed to gut three fresh sea breams with his right hand, using the fingers emerging from his cast to weigh down the fish.

"Sure you don't want help with that?" Santiago asked him.

"I'm good." Luc dumped their murky gray entrails into a food composter. He turned off the sink's tap and rolled up the large fish in paper towels before packing them into the refrigerator for cooking later.

Meanwhile, Eric dumped a bag of wet, black spiky sea urchins into a colander to rinse as Santiago squeezed lemon juice into the ceviche marinade. Next, Eric cut openings in each urchin, prying the bright yellow gonads from the shell with a spoon. They looked a bit like scrambled eggs.

Santiago picked up an onion to dice. Without looking up, Eric passed him a sharp chef's knife. It was as if the three men spoke a common language and understood the delicate choreography of moving around each other in a cramped kitchen.

It was the first time Luc felt he could let his guard down around Eric.

CHAPTER 37

Iris looked up from her iPad as she saw Luc approaching the casita. He looked happier than he'd been since he'd broken his arm a week before. "How did the cooking class go?"

"It was awesome. I'm going to be fantasizing about those amazing ingredients for a long time."

Her eyebrows danced upwards. "*Those* are your fantasies?"

Luc laughed. "Not my only ones. But wait 'til you taste the sea bream. Oh, Eric asked if we'd sit with them at dinner so we could debrief over the meal. That okay?"

"You guys are besties now?"

"Only as fellow chefs. Other than that, he's still a douche. Plenty of that in any kitchen. You and Tia can talk, so you don't have to listen to us."

"Sure, we foodie widows can hang out while you two talk shop." Iris rose and flicked on the veranda light. "You'd better hurry and change for dinner."

Iris spotted the Duvals as soon as she and Luc entered the pavilion. Kelly and Lisa rushed over, looking conspiratorial.

"Sara Jane suggested we dig up more background about Cal and

Kenneth," Kelly said. "So, we figured we'd sit with Margo and Kenneth tonight. Do you want to pump Sierra and Cal for some more details?"

"We had dinner with Margo and Kenneth last night, but I don't think we learned anything relevant to the situation." Luc looked to Iris for confirmation, and she shook her head in agreement. "Why don't we compare notes tomorrow?" Then Luc explained that they were already tied up for tonight's dinner.

They agreed to talk later and turned their attention to locating their dinner partners.

On a detour to the bar, Iris whispered to Luc, "Are you sure you want to encourage them?"

"Did I sound too eager to help?"

"You didn't sound *dis*couraging." When they reached the polished counter in front of Sammy, Iris ordered a pomegranate margarita. At that moment, they heard a voice calling out.

"Hey, chef! Here you are." Eric approached with a cocky strut. "Ready for the big reveal?"

Luc lifted his fresh glass of beer from the counter. "Let's find out how we did as sous-chefs."

Tia trailed behind Eric, looking chic in yet another vintage outfit, but appearing lost.

"I guess we'll need to amuse ourselves tonight," Iris said to her.

"Nothing new," Tia said cheerfully.

The mellow salsa background music faded out as the foursome headed to their table.

Iris felt a bit bad for Tia. A few days before, when she was convinced that Luc wanted to break up with her, she thought she'd be in Tia's position—running out the clock on a dying relationship. So, when Tia said, "I heard about the podcast from Kelly. What's the latest?" Iris didn't have the heart to discourage her interest. The men were already engaged in conversation, anyway.

"Did she tell you about the profiler?" Iris asked.

"Yeah. But I can't picture Kenneth as some big mastermind. He strikes me as a type who's all bluff and appearance."

"He told us last night that he trades cattle futures," Iris said.

"Is that a real thing? It sounds fake, like trading pork belly futures."

"Uh, that one actually *is* a real thing. In fact, both are real."

"Anyway, Cal seems like a better bet," Tia said. "He's very much a take charge kind of guy. And the scar makes him look badass. I wonder how he got it."

"It probably makes him seem more sinister than he really is. He and Sierra seem to be trying to help the people here, not take advantage of them. I can't imagine him killing Julio."

"Didn't Cal used to be on the pro surfing circuit? Traveling around the world, getting all his boards and equipment through customs would be a perfect cover for smuggling a few priceless souvenirs along the way."

"I hadn't thought of that." Iris looked over now to where Sierra and Cal were quietly chatting at a small table. "It seems like the police have some evidence tying this resort to the thefts. Sure, Julio worked here, but it feels like there's more to it than that. I don't think they came here to question Luc and me just because we were the last ones to see the Crying Crocodile."

"Maybe it has something to do with that hut Luc found in the jungle behind the far beach. Or the cigarette boat he saw."

"Wait! What hut?" She couldn't believe Luc had told Tia something about the case that he hadn't told her. She glared at him and kicked his shin under the table.

"Ouch!" Luc shot Iris a questioning, injured look.

"What's this hut you told Tia about?" Iris asked him.

Luc deflected the question with a mouthed, "Later."

She restrained herself from kicking him again because the server arrived with their appetizers.

Their table was soon piled high with servings of sea urchin ceviche, bowls of tomato coconut soup, and roasted beet salad. This reduced the conversation to contented sounds of appreciation.

CHAPTER 38

The next morning, Iris stared at her tired face in the bathroom mirror while randomly slapping on sunblock. It took a moment to remember why she was mad at Luc. They'd had a fight in their casita the night before and ended up sleeping on opposite sides of the bed. Luc had admitted to venturing into the jungle to investigate a hut he'd seen from the beach but told her he'd only gone a few steps in before turning back. He mentioned it to Tia because she was the first person he ran into when he got back to the resort, and he explained he didn't tell Iris because he was afraid she'd overreact.

When Iris responded jaguars can run fifty miles an hour and kill a human by piercing their brain with their teeth, Luc shot back with "That's why I didn't go in any further. I thought better of taking the risk. Unlike you on that day I got a phone call from the FBI saying that you'd been drugged and kidnapped."

She snapped, "But I hadn't willingly put myself in that position." *At least not that time.*

Iris rubbed more sunblock lotion on her legs. Who was she kidding? She was relieved to have Luc experience for himself the excitement of getting sucked into crime-solving, as long as he didn't get himself killed. The adrenaline high of taking a few risks—there was nothing like it. Then, hopefully, he'd get off her case. She never looked for trouble—it just had a way of finding her. Her mind and analytical training made her good at observing details and putting the pieces of a puzzle together.

But for this case here in Costa Rica, she intended to keep her head down. She'd show Luc that she could resist the temptation to meddle. Let *him* be the one to get dragged in by his curiosity.

She heard a faint rustling of sheets from back in the bedroom. Luc perched on the edge of the bed, facing away from her, his hair sticking up in all directions. He turned toward her, his expression contrite. "I'm sorry, babe. I should have told you about the damn hut. It was hypocritical of me to go into the jungle after criticizing you for taking risks. I don't want this to be a fight, okay?"

"Apology accepted." Iris leaned against the doorframe. "Now let's get dressed. I'm dying for some coffee."

Ten minutes later, they were leaving the casita and ran into Kelly on the path. She was out of breath from her early morning run, her Oregon State T-shirt stained with perspiration. "I found the hut!" she called out.

Iris shot Luc a dirty look. *Am I the only one who doesn't know about this hut?*

Kelly continued, "I was too scared to stay long, and the door was locked, but I found something on the ground nearby." She held out a small fragment of pottery, the size of a thumbnail, in her flat palm. "Is this a clue?"

Luc turned it over in his hand. It was tan-colored clay with a tiny section of glossy green finish in one corner. "Maybe. Where was this?"

"In the dirt outside the door. I almost missed it, but that little splotch of green caught my eye," Kelly said.

"I wish we knew the purpose of that hut." Iris said as she held the piece up to the light.

"Let's ask Sierra," Kelly suggested.

"No," Luc said. "We don't want anyone to know you were poking around there. It could be dangerous."

"Especially if Cal's the one behind the thefts," Iris said.

Kelly wrapped the shard in a tissue and stuffed it into the pocket of her shorts.

"Wait," Iris said. "Could I see that again?"

Kelly unwrapped the clay fragment and handed it to Iris. "Hang on. I'll be right back."

A few minutes later, Iris emerged from the casita holding one of the bowls she'd purchased in Santa Elena. She held up the chip of the pottery next to the bowl. The surfaces matched.

"Is this a common glaze color?" Kelly asked. "Or is it distinctive to the studio you visited?"

"I think this green is Violetta's own mix, but I could be wrong," Iris said. "By the way, did you learn anything interesting about Kenneth last night at dinner?"

"I learned more than I wanted to know about trading cattle futures. What a boring job." Kelly sighed loudly. "Mom asked if he travels much out of the country, and he said hardly ever. Chicago and Houston are his home bases. He sometimes vacations in Cabo, but that's about it."

"Hmm. Doesn't sound like he fits Dr. Fred's profile," Luc said. "Unless he's lying about not travelling internationally."

"But we did learn something that surprised me about Margo. Kenneth let it slip that she has a son about my age. She seemed kind of embarrassed about it."

"Sure. Middle-aged Mom doesn't fit with the sexy babe vibe she's trying to send out." Iris said. "Margo must have had the kid when she was really young."

"Not that the information helps us with our sleuthing," Kelly said. "We're going to sit with Cal and Sierra tonight at dinner. It looks like Cal might be moving into the front-runner position as a suspect."

"Be careful, Kelly." Luc warned. "This isn't a game. In fact, you should let the cops do the investigating. Whoever it is, this person has killed someone."

"Don't worry. Mom and I will be very, very subtle."

CHAPTER 39

Iris couldn't stop wondering what Violetta's pottery workshop could have to do with the spectacular, and now murderous, artifact thefts. As she and Luc finished the last crumbs of their delicious breakfast pastries, she said, "I think we're making a mystery out of nothing. That hut is probably used for storage for the resort. The clay fragment might have broken off a vase that's no longer needed in a casita."

Luc poured himself more coffee and held up the carafe. "Want a refill?"

She shook her head.

"It seems a little remote for ordinary storage. You'd think they could build a structure on site." Luc said. "Plus, do we know that the resort even owns that land?"

"I could ask Guillermo. He seems like a straightforward good guy."

"No, don't. We shouldn't take anyone off the suspect list yet. I saw someone's footprints leading back toward the hut, so someone is motivated enough to get there to take the risk of waking up a cranky jaguar."

"Should we say anything to those O.I.J. officers?"

"Like what? What evidence do we have linking the hut to any crime?"

"You're right. Kelly is getting us all worked up, and we need to let it go." Iris grabbed her phone as it vibrated itself across the table. "Elvis, hi. Is my search history cleaned up?"

"I had no idea you'd been mixed up in so much cool shit! You even got arrested!"

"Falsely arrested."

"And those other cases—murders and intrigue. I wasn't able to get rid of everything, but I buried your secrets pretty deep. There's only one thing."

"Yes?"

"You said a podcaster was showcasing an antiquity looting case that's happening near where you are now?"

Iris gritted her teeth. "Tell me she didn't find my search history before you deleted it?"

"This Sara Jane McClinnock person evidently found the bank robbery accusation before I could deep-six it. The one where the guard was shot. She's calling you a 'person of interest' in this new case."

"Oh, no!"

"It gets worse. She's flying down there to investigate things in person."

CHAPTER 40

Text messages between Sara Jane McClinnock and Devin Crowley Sat 1-02-24:

SJM

Dev, any word back from our followers with connections in Costa Rica? Need to find out why investigation seems to focus on that resort! Must be more than just museum guard worked there and thefts were in neighboring villages. I think I remember a woman from the comments section last year who retired to this area. See if you can ferret out her contacts.

Plane lands this afternoon and will rent car to visit villages. I'll try to pry info out of locals but need you to work your end as well. Keep looking for similar robberies from small museums. Check Europe, US, South/Central America. Am cc'ing you my notes with leads to follow on guests, etc.

DC

Rings a bell about that ex-pat follower in Costa Rica. I'll DM her and see if she can get us some inside info. Will you be able to record a show tonight so I can air it tomorrow at the usual time?

> SJM
>
> Yes. Will write script on plane/ interview some guests at resort. Already prepared notes.
>
> DC

NOTES ON SARA JANE MCCLINNOCK'S IPHONE:

PACK: Pop filter, 2 mics, stand, extra headphones + sunblock/bug spray!

    SAT 1-02-24: United flt.1120 leaves O'Hare at **9:30**/arrives Liberia @ **1:35** (set time back 1 hr). Resort plane meets me for 1 hr. flt. Pick up Jeep at Alamo in Nosara.

INTERVIEWEES:

1. **KELLY AND LISA DUVAL** (initial contacts): Mother/daughter vineyard owners from Napa. Have them describe visit to Santa Elena/ their reactions to discovery of theft of Crying Croc + murder of guard. Unlikely suspects.
2. **SIERRA + CAL WINTERS**: (resort owners) talk re starting the resort/why here/supporting local businesses/ background on the dead pool guy — his personality, family, friends I can interview? How common is violent crime in this region? Draw out Cal (fits profile-60ish) and learn about his background as professional surfer, where he traveled on the circuit (similar crimes in those locs—Devin?) Ask him details about the antiquities to see how informed he is. Wife was/is yoga instructor. Sound her out on the thefts + value of the pieces. Ask re the jewels. Are they suspects? **NOTE**: Kelly says Iris Reid has photo of Crying Croc on her phone. Get this!
3. **IRIS REID AND LUC CORMIER**: Iris doesn't fit profile but has history of involvement in crimes/murders around Boston. In 2022 was accused of robbing a bank where guard was shot,

but apparently was mistaken i.d.—**Similarity to this crime a co-incidence**? Runs small architecture firm in Cambridge. Reason for so many overlaps with criminal cases? Undercover agent? Criminal? How to dig out? She's definitely a person of interest. They were last ones to see Crying Croc other than museum peeps. Luc= chef boyfriend, owns big-deal restaurant in Cambridge. Check on its financials. Seems harmless per Kelly. Too young for profile (late 30s). Broke arm in surfing accident last week. Witnessed cigarette boat at night/furtive loading package from beach + found hut in jungle. Need to investigate boat/hut's possible relationship to crime. Ask them about visit from OIJ agents. What were they asked? Why single them out? (b/c last ones to see cc?)
4. KENNETH NICHOLS AND MARGO WILLIAMS: He fits profile. 50ish. Divorced 2x with 4 kids to support. Heavy drinker. Trades cattle futures in Houston. Kelly says travel mainly to Chicago and Cabo but have Devin verify. Business school contacts? Connections in Mexico? Ask him about pre-Columbian art.Margo=gallery owner girlfriend. Kelly says super-sexed, coming on to all the men. Also, heavy drinker. Possible gallery connection to pre-Columbian art? Only one not here for the surfing program.
5. ERIC SCHWARTZ AND TIA MOSS: he's restaurant owner/chef for Twigs in L.A. Very type A, acc. to Kelly. Big ego. Pushy. 40ish=young for profile but might fit. Media makes him sound like workaholic. Probably not a suspect. Tia is graphic designer in L.A. with small firm. Works with restaurants + hotels to design graphics, logos. Unlikely suspect.
6. MATEO AND GUILLERMO: Find out last names. Surf instructors. Live in Santa Elena. Guillermo is mid 30s, married. Mateo is early 20s, unmarried. Flesh out their backgrounds and pump for info re pool guy.

TIMELINE ON THEFTS:

Quartet of pre-Hispanic (around 500 BCE) jade incense burners incorporating an animal with a valuable jewel, each stolen from a separate village.

Final robbery escalated to include murder of night watchman, Julio Alvarez.

1. December 18: the **Leaping Jaguar** of Maquenco with **sapphire** on chain around neck
2. December 21: the **Dancing Serpent** of Mafambu with **ruby** embedded in its tail
3. December 25: the **Hunting Eagle** of Garza with **lapis lazuli** clutched in talons
4. December 30: the **Crying Crocodile** of Santa Elena with **emerald** as a tear

BACKGROUND ON THE QUARTET FROM ONLINE *TICO TIMES* VIA DEVON:

The renowned Tica Archaeologist Ramón Santos discovered a cache of buried artifacts in 1991 when he was excavating the Dolce Nombre site for relics from around 500 BCE. The Mayans were not thought to have lived as far south as Costa Rica, but other indigenous peoples did inhabit the area. These tribes were influenced by cultures from what is now Colombia and they displayed sophisticated engineering skills which can be seen at the Guayabo ruins.

Instead of handing his finds over to the Museo Nacional de Costa Rica, Ramón Santos chose to distribute the antiquities, including the quartet of jeweled incense burners, among the nearest four villages in order to allow the locals closer access to their priceless cultural heritage.

CHAPTER 41

Iris was balancing her weight on her arms, and slowly raising her legs in front of her, when the clatter of a suitcase rolling along the path nearby broke her concentration.

Next to her, Sierra continued to guide Luc in an adaptation. "Move into warrior pose 2. That's right. Now rest your cast on top of your head and press your right forearm on top of it. This should stretch out your shoulders."

Iris craned her neck toward the newcomer and promptly collapsed on her side. Guillermo was leading a young woman with a bright red bob and a huge straw hat past the yoga platform. From the thuds on the various mats around Iris, the six other yogis had also lost their focus on the firefly pose.

Sierra noticed the disturbance and turned toward the visitor. "You must be Sara Jane. I'm Sierra Winters. We spoke on the phone. Welcome to La Guaria Morada Resort. I hope you had an easy trip from Chicago."

The young woman's voice ("Escaping winter is worth all the travel.") was surprisingly deep and sultry with a hint of Midwestern broad vowels. "I appreciate you letting me join the session in the middle."

"My husband, Cal, and I look forward to hearing your podcasts about the resort. We'd be happy to fill you in on its history tonight at dinner. Now I'll let Guillermo take you to your casita so you can freshen up. Cocktails are in the main pavilion at six."

Kelly cut her eyes over to Iris, brows raised.

Sara Jane and Guillermo disappeared down the path, and Sierra glanced at her watch. "Let's finish up with a spinal twist, followed by a few moments in corpse pose."

After their final Namastes, and the students had stashed their mats and blocks in a storage bin, Iris made a beeline for Kelly. "It sounds like Sierra thinks Sara Jane is here to do a travel podcast on the resort."

Kelly grimaced. "She's going to be so mad when she finds out the truth."

That evening, Iris and Luc showed up at the dining pavilion curious about whether Sara Jane could pull off interviewing guests under false pretenses. "I can't imagine Cal and Sierra will let her stay once they find out she wants to grill the guests, and themselves, as suspects in a murder-cum-robbery," Iris said. "Especially with over two thousand followers listening. Then again, they say all PR is good PR."

Luc looked over at the bar. "There she is. She looks younger than I expected."

Young, but self-confident, judging from her body language.

Sara Jane was clearly charming Kenneth while Margo looked on, her eyes shooting daggers. Sara Jane wore a short, checkered dress that, along with a smattering of freckles across the bridge of her nose, projected an innocent schoolgirl look. She had a bag slung over her shoulder that looked like it might even contain lesson books. All three of them held layered, iridescent-looking cocktails in tall hurricane glasses.

"And you're already surfing theses waves, Kenneth? After only one week?" Sara Jane said. "You must be very athletic. Do you do other sports back home in Houston?"

She's good. Maybe she will be able to pull off this charade.

Iris and Luc moved to the other end of the bar, and Luc leaned toward Sammy. "What is in that drink they have?"

"It's called a Rainbow Paradise. It's got blue curacao, pineapple juice with coconut rum, and grenadine."

"Is it any good?" Iris asked.

Sammy shrugged. "It's fruity and packs a wallop."

Sara Jane let out a surprisingly loud, bawdy laugh at something Kenneth said. "Call me S.J. Everyone does."

"Chardonnay for me, please," Iris said. They'd need to keep their heads clear around this woman. Luc ordered a Corona with a lime.

By the time they had gathered up their drinks, Sierra had swooped in and was leading S.J. away from the bar, over toward Cal, who was smiling warmly at the newest guest.

Tia sidled up to the bar next to Iris and Luc and asked Sammy for another mojito.

"Where's Eric?" Luc asked.

"He's visiting the kitchen." Tia looked at Luc. "Just what the chef-in-charge loves when he's preparing dinner for eleven, am I right?"

Luc shuddered.

"Have you been introduced yet to Rebecca of Sunnybrook Farm?" Tia asked.

Iris snorted. "Not yet. Have you? Did she try to convince you she's a travel podcaster?"

"She left it vague, said she was writing about the resort. Oh, look. She's gotten out her mic and laptop. I guess the interviews are starting."

Sierra and Cal were sitting across from S.J. at a corner table set apart from the others. Two floor lamps lit them from either side. S.J. set two mics into telescoping stands and attached their cables to her computer. She laid a black box with an array of knobs and sliders next to her. Sierra moved a flower centerpiece off to one side.

"Okay," Tia said. "Let's watch Cal's and Sierra's expressions to see if we can spot the exact moment it dawns on them what S.J. is actually here for."

"Don't sell S.J. short. I'm guessing she's a pretty good actress." Iris said. "But what amazes me is why Sierra and Cal didn't look up her podcast online before she came."

"Yeah," Luc added. "It's called *Real Crimes in Real Time*. That should have given them a clue."

Over the next twenty minutes, Iris, Luc and Tia subtly tried to observe the interview, stealing little glances from their perch by the bar. Iris noticed Kelly and Lisa doing the same thing from a table in the opposite corner. Only Kenneth and Margo seemed oblivious, absorbed in their private conversation.

"Have you listened to her first podcast for this series?" Iris asked Tia.

"No. Did she say anything about us?"

"Luc and I played it after lunch when we heard she was coming. It's basically setting the stage with information about the artifacts and the thefts with some speculative information about the murder. S.J. tasks her listeners with finding inside intel about the case. Evidently, she even has listeners down here in Costa Rica. The second episode is supposed to air tomorrow."

"Oh, God," moaned Tia. "Does this mean they're going to dig up dirt on all of *us*?"

Iris eyed her thoughtfully. "Why? How much dirt do *you* have buried?"

CHAPTER 42

After the interview with Sierra and Cal, which S.J. felt she'd pulled off without exposing her real agenda, she'd moved to Kelly and Lisa's table for dinner. It was a relief to be herself again with them, with no need to keep her story straight. How much time did she have to investigate here before Sierra and Cal kicked her out?

S.J. had resisted opening the text that had pinged on her phone during dinner until she was back in her casita. Once there, she took off her ridiculous dress and flopped down on the bed, finally comfortable. She opened her laptop and read the text from Devin.

Text messages between Sara Jane McClinnock and Devin Crowley Sat 1-02-24:

DC

> We've lucked out! Samantha King, our ex-pat retiree who now lives in Costa Rica just happens to have a son-in-law (Raf Luz) in the Costa Rican police in Nosara. She DM'd me back after quizzing him about the case.

> The OIJ has jurisdiction, that's the separate investigative branch of the police, but Raf had heard rumors that, after the murder, the police found a text on Julio's phone to his cousin, a masseuse at the resort.

> It said that the "Big boss" was staying at the resort this week, and that if anything happened to him, Julio, she should go into hiding.
>
> The cops are trying to find evidence about who this "Big boss" is, but it's got to be one of the guests.

SJM

OMG! That's the link! Bless this Samantha King and her relatives! Now we know why the cops are zeroing in on the resort! So where is this masseuse? I want to interview her.

DC

> You can't. No one can find her. The morning after Julio was killed, she disappeared. Can you blame her?
>
> Either Julio didn't know who the BB was, or he didn't want to endanger her by telling her the name.

SJM

That still narrows the suspects down to eight. Lets off Sierra and Cal. Rats.

I kind of liked him for it and got some suspicious remarks recorded before dinner. But better to avoid dead ends.

And I don't want to get kicked out of this place for falsely accusing the owner of murder. I'm sure they'll find me out soon enough.

So, what's the masseuse's name?

DC

> Don't know. You should be able to get that from your Napa sources.
>
> And aren't the suspects narrowed down to six? You don't think Kelly and Lisa are involved, do you?

SJM

Never say never.

I wonder why BB would come down here now? The other thefts happened over the last few weeks. Has BB been down here all that time? Or orchestrating this from afar and planning to fly in for the finale?

DC

Maybe BB wants to tie up loose ends after he gets his hands on the final artifact. Leave no trail behind, right?

SJM

Maybe. I need to think about this and rewrite my script tonight. I'll have to see what I can extract out of the Sierra and Cal interview to use in the podcast for tomorrow.

DC

Okay, I'll let you get to it. If anything important comes in through the DMs, I'll shoot you a text.

Check your email for the attachments I sent with the preliminary reports on the guests. I used our usual sources.

I'll air whatever you send me at the regular time tomorrow.

SJM

Thanks, Dev. You're a star!

DC

CHAPTER 43

The next day after breakfast, Iris was surprised to see S.J. on the beach, ready to join the surf class. She was really leaning into her cover as a genuine travel writer. Her skin looked painfully white and ready to burn compared to the rest of them with their deepening tans.

"I hope you've got industrial-strength sunblock on," Tia said to S.J. as they waxed their surfboards.

"I know—this white skin glows in the dark."

"While I disappear in the dark, a useful trait." Tia winked at her. Tia and Iris dragged their boards over to the water's edge. Behind them, Guillermo explained to S.J. how to practice her pop ups on land.

Iris and Tia paddled through the whitewater on their stomachs, closing their eyes as the small inshore waves sprayed them.

Iris turned to her. "So, do you like surfing more?"

"Yeah, now that my standing up ratio is higher. How 'bout you?"

"This trip was Luc's idea, but now that I can ride a big wave in to shore, surfing gives me a rush. I'd be less enthused if we were bobbing around in the freezing water off Massachusetts, wetsuit or not."

"Yeah, even the ocean off L.A. isn't as warm as this. I don't think I'll be seeking out the rad barrels there."

Iris laughed. "Has Mateo has been teaching you surf slang?"

"I'm no hodad or paddlepuss, girl. The nugs are peeling. Let's get out there!"

Two hours later, when Iris finally emerged from the water and wearily dragged her board up onto the sand, she heard S.J. complaining to Guillermo about how sore her arms were after this first lesson. "Does the resort have a masseuse?"

"Not at the moment," he answered. "I think Sierra is looking for a new one."

"Could I get in touch with the old one? See if she'd be willing to come give me a massage in my casita? I'd make it worth her while."

Guillermo shook his head. "I have no idea where Ana went. None of us know. Her cousin, Julio, was her only family, and he recently… passed away."

Why does S.J. want to contact Ana? Is the masseuse part of this crime puzzle?

After lunch, Iris and Luc rushed back to their casita to listen to the second episode of S.J.'s podcast. They stretched out on the bed with the iPad propped up in front of them.

For the next half hour, S.J.'s sultry radio voice mesmerized them.

The podcaster first recapped the crimes for her audience. Then she confided, "I have learned from a confidential source why the police believe the mastermind behind the thefts and murder may be a guest at a certain resort in Costa Rica."

Iris sucked in her breath. At least S.J. didn't name La Guaria Morada.

"In order to protect this contact—"

"Ha! Like she's Woodward or Bernstein," Iris muttered.

"…we can't go into any specifics about this sensitive link, so you'll have to take my word for it. These are descriptions of the eight suspects."

Iris and Luc were relieved when S.J. didn't use any of their real names. She called Luc a popular chef and restauranteur in the Boston area. From her sources, she'd learned that he was a workaholic—

Luc sat up indignantly and snorted.

"… with little extracurricular time and no criminal record. But, as we know, restaurants are risky businesses requiring a lot of capital. And they often have immigrant labor in the kitchen, possibly Costa Ricans who might have known about the artifacts. The chef is in his late 30s, younger than the profile Dr. Fred had put together, but profiles are not always reliable."

S.J. went on: "We've learned that a week ago, this Boston chef was out on a nearby beach at midnight. He noticed a cigarette boat approaching the shore. A figure handed something to someone on the boat before it sped off and the figure disappeared. The question is, why was the chef on the beach at night?"

Iris and Luc swore in tandem.

S.J. moved on to the chef's girlfriend, an architect in the Boston area as well. Being female, she also didn't fit the profile, but she had some interesting skeletons in her closet. S.J. went on to list them in a slightly disguised manner.

Iris sputtered and made objections from her side of the bed. Luc pointed out, "At least she didn't say we were from Cambridge. That would have made it easier to identify us."

"The architect's attorney brother repeatedly gets her released from these incidents, so perhaps that has given her a sense of invulnerability," S.J. conjectured. "In addition, as an architect, she might appreciate these artifacts for their beauty, and want to acquire them for her private collection. Or maybe our architect wants to branch out and reset the jewels into a new piece of jewelry of her own design."

Iris pressed *pause* on the podcast. "Is anyone going to believe this nonsense?"

"You mean her thousands of listeners or the police? I hope none of them do. You know, this might affect both of our businesses. Our identities aren't very well hidden. A few crazies can do a lot of damage." Luc rolled over onto his back and stuffed two pillows under his head. "Let's hear what she's dug up on the others. Hopefully she moves on to a better theory than I need money for my restaurant, and you've been involved in a few suspicious cases in the past. Oh, but I do like her speculation that you have a magical sense of invulnerability."

Iris stuck out her tongue at him and pressed *play*. As S.J. discussed the other three couples, Iris and Luc learned a few new interesting facts:

1. While Kelly and Lisa ("the mother-daughter duo from Napa") were the ones who'd brought the museum robberies and murder to S.J.'s attention, and were not seriously considered suspects, Lisa's husband (Kelly's father) had been killed two years before in an unsolved hit-and-run. Although unlikely, this might be somehow connected to the crimes.
2. Kenneth ("the Texan financier") was paying alimony and child support to two ex-wives with four children between them. Trading cattle futures can be highly speculative, and Kenneth has lately been in a slump.

Margo ("the Texan gift shop owner") has an unemployed twenty-three-year-old son from her first marriage living with her. While art galleries can be a notorious source of money laundering, Margo's store is more of a high-priced gift shop than a place to buy serious artwork. She sells large, glazed pots from Mexico, fancy tableware and pricey candles. The shop is apparently doing quite well.

1. Eric ("the L.A. chef") is branching out from his popular restaurant in Santa Monica and has bought an expensive second space in downtown L.A. His contractors gutted the building six months ago but were issued a Stop Order from the building department for violating legal working hours. It seems that Eric was trying to rush the renovation and now the project is stalled, which can't be cheap. Would this cause him to resort to desperate measures?
2. Tia ("the L.A. graphic designer") seemed to be just what she claimed, a small-scale graphic designer. She alone seems to have no secrets or questionable debts in her past, at least none they've discovered yet.

At the end of the podcast, Luc ran his free hand through his hair. "Whoa. I feel bad for Eric."

Iris jumped to her feet and stared at him. "Babe, I feel bad for all of us. We came here for a vacation. Not to have our lives dissected by this libelous bitch in front of thousands of voyeurs!"

Luc tilted his head to one side. "Technically, it's only libel if it's untrue."

Iris threw a pillow at him. He caught it. "And I think you're missing the more important point."

"Okay, enlighten me."

"According to S.J.'s analysis, there's a murderer here among our small group."

CHAPTER 44

S.J. hadn't bothered to unpack her suitcase the day before. She figured that once today's podcast went on the air, she'd have burned her bridges at the resort. Even if, by some miracle, Cal and Sierra were too busy to listen to it, at least one guest would hear it and storm in to the owner's office demanding her banishment.

But it couldn't be helped. Her followers expected new material twice a week and if she didn't throw them raw meat, she'd lose them.

S.J. had squeezed the water out of her bathing suit and thrown it in a plastic bag when she heard a knock on her casita door. It was ten minutes after the podcast had ended, and Sierra stood in her doorway, a look of cold fury on her face.

"You deceived us, Sara Jane, and you need to leave. Now. You can drive to the next town where you can find someplace else to stay. Or head straight to the airport. Your choice." Sierra banged the door on her way out. So much for the chill yoga guru.

Luckily, S.J. had a back-up plan. Samantha King, her follower in this region had volunteered to let S.J. stay in her guest room. She zipped up her suitcase and headed out to her rental car in the parking lot.

SJM

Well, that didn't take long. The owners kicked me out of the resort. I'm heading over to Samantha's now. At least my 24 hours at ground zero gave me a chance to clamp eyes on all the suspects. And staying with Samantha will hopefully give me more access to her cop son-in-law and any developments from the federal police.

DC

Ouch! Hope the booting wasn't too dramatic. The things we do for journalism. 😊

We got a lot of feedback on the episode that dropped today.

We're already getting responses from your call for information.

Someone says they have some dirt valuable intel on Iris Reid. You can see it on the forum.

Do you think Reid could be BB?

SJM

Maybe. Let me grill talk to Samantha and see what the cops have dug up.

DC

Hope she has nice digs. I'll get contact details by DM.

Okay to forward them? I'll filter out the whack jobs. 👌

SJM

Good work, Dev. Gotta go.

CHAPTER 45

Iris stared at Luc, who was still leaning up against the bed's carved headboard. "You're right—S.J. is claiming one of the other six guests stole the urns and killed Julio. Or at least had accomplices do the dirty work. Are we in danger?" she asked. "If we're not in the way of this person getting what they want, does that make us safe? That damn S.J. told the Big boss you saw the cigarette boat which may be how the crying crocodile was smuggled out. That might make you a threat."

Luc stood up and walked over to his suitcase, lying open on a wooden stand. "Iris, we need to leave. Let's pack our things and get a ride to the Nosara Airport. We can stay in a hotel there if we have to wait for a flight."

Iris locked her hands on top of her head. "I can't believe this! I was just getting good at surfing." She moved toward her suitcase, then stopped. "What if S.J. is bullshitting about the mastermind being a guest here? She could be making up stuff about a secret source to keep her listeners' attention."

Luc, holding several shirts still on their hangers, turned around from the closet to look at her. "Are you willing to take that chance? Someone who's murdered before may be staying in the casita next to ours."

Iris shuddered. "No, you're right." She moved into the bathroom and scooped her array of cosmetics into a case. The phone in her pocket buzzed. She checked the screen. A text from Kelly read,

> "Did you hear the podcast? What should we do?"

Iris showed the text to Luc, who responded, "How do we know Kelly and Lisa aren't the masterminds? Calling in a podcaster might have been a smokescreen."

"Really? Kelly and Lisa? They seem so…harmless."

Luc arched his brows. "Don't underestimate this person, or persons. They've already gotten away with a lot, and none of it by being conspicuous."

Iris texted Kelly back.

> We heard it. Not sure what to do. Any ideas?

She showed the screen to Luc before pressing <send>.

As they finished packing, there was a knock on the door. Sierra stood there looking wan. As she noticed their zipped-up suitcases, she seemed to wince. "I don't know if you heard S.J.'s podcast, but we've sent her away for her blatant invasion of everyone's privacy. Cal and I are so sorry for the way our local tragedy has affected your vacation. We are going to waive half the cost of your stay because of this inconvenience. Lieutenant Alvarez from the OIJ is here now and would like to speak to all the guests in the pavilion."

Inconvenience? There's a gross understatement!

"We'll see you in the pavilion in a few minutes." Sierra turned and left.

Luc checked his watch. "Well, it's probably too late to catch any flights out today, anyway."

A few moments later, as Iris and Luc filed into the pavilion, she noticed that each of the other couples was keeping to themselves, casting furtive, suspicious glances as they sat at the various tables set for two. S.J. had revealed a lot of embarrassing personal information.

Only Kelly offered them a tentative smile. Tia looked despondent, although that could be because of her disillusionment with Eric.

Lieutenant Alvarez stood in front of the bar, quietly facing the guests. Officer Diaz and Cal flanked him like soldiers at parade rest. Sierra sat at a nearby table, massaging a temple. Iris was surprised to see Guillermo and Mateo clustered by the kitchen door with Chef Vargas. The room was deadly quiet. Even Margo kept her mouth closed as she and Kenneth sat stiffly, bodies angled away from each other.

"Many of you have heard about the recent thefts from nearby museums and the murder of a resort staff member while he was moonlighting as a guard in his home village." Alvarez began. "Today, an American podcaster claimed to have inside information on our investigation and is targeting the perpetrator as someone staying here now at this resort."

Iris glanced around at everyone's expressions but could detect nothing revealing.

"While I cannot say anything about our ongoing investigation, I can assure you that you are in no more danger here now than you were last week when you arrived." Alvarez looked over at Cal. A muscle clenched in the resort owner's jaw as he offered a not-so-reassuring smile.

What double-speak! We didn't know we were in danger then.

"We hope to follow up on a number of very solid leads and tie up our case quite soon. Meanwhile, Officer Diaz will remain at the resort to ensure your safety. We'd prefer that you all stay here together under his watch. Please enjoy the rest of your stay."

Alvarez gave a small bow before heading out of the pavilion. After the door closed, Cal moved into the central spot and made a slight attention-getting cough. "Sierra and I would like to offer our sincerest apologies for any awkwardness caused by Ms. McClinnock's invasion of your lives on her podcast. If we hadn't been so distracted by Julio's tragic death and these local museum thefts, we would have researched her request for a visit more thoroughly. She has been sent away and will bother none of you again while you're here."

At this point, Sierra stood and joined Cal. "I'd like to add my own apology for any stress Ms. McClinnock may have caused. This is your vacation, and a time to relax while you learn an exciting new sport. Cal and I are crushed that the positive spirit of this two-week session has been disturbed. As I mentioned to you in your casitas, we will refund half of the cost of your stay. I hope you will all remain for the rest of the session, and we can restore the convivial atmosphere we've all been enjoying."

Iris thought Sierra's eyes looked red from crying, and she felt a pang of sympathy. S.J. had screwed over the resort owners as well as the guests. The resort could get disastrous reviews on the travel websites, or even get Cal and Sierra sued for allowing access to the malevolent podcaster.

Iris looked at Luc. "Should we stay?"

Luc blew out a breath, considering. Just then, Chef Vargas approached their table. "I hope you'll finish out the session, Luc. I'd love to have you join me in the kitchen again to talk more shop."

Iris was startled by the chef's deep, resonant voice. She hadn't had any occasion before to speak with him directly. But it was not the first time she had heard that voice.

CHAPTER 46

Shortly after Cal and Sierra finished their plea for the guests to stay, Iris and Luc left the pavilion and headed back to their casita, avoiding Kelly's questions with a promise to text her.

Locking the door behind her for the first time, Iris hovered at the bedroom door, eyeing their packed suitcases. "What did Alvarez mean when he said he'd prefer we all stay here under his watch? Was that like saying 'don't leave town'? Do we have a choice?"

Luc dropped into a rattan lounge chair and nervously itched the inside of his cast. "I'm wondering if we need to call the resort lawyer, Mark Harris. I don't like this set-up. You and I can't get caught up in a bogus scandal just to amuse some podcast audience."

Iris perched on the arm of the chair facing Luc. "Alvarez didn't confirm S.J.'s 'inside information' about the mysterious mastermind being a guest here."

"But he must suspect something if he's leaving an officer here to keep an eye on us."

"Who could the bad guy be? Kenneth? Eric?"

"Why do you assume it's a guy? Maybe it's Tia or Margo?"

"Good point," Iris agreed. "That S.J. couldn't dig up any dirt on Tia is suspicious in itself. She seems almost too good to be true."

After a few moments, Luc pounded a fist on the arm of his chair. "This is so messed up! First, I break my arm and can't surf, and now some local crime is screwing up the rest of our vacation. I'd wanted to at least spend some time talking with Santiago about recipes."

Iris sat up excitedly. "That reminds me—when I heard Chef Vargas talking with you in the pavilion, I recognized his voice. He was the one I overheard arguing with Julio in Spanish when I was having my massage. Remember, I asked you what peligroso meant? I Google-translated it to mean dangerous. I think Chef Vargas was warning him not to do something that was too dangerous. Could he have known that the master thief was at the resort?"

"Why didn't you tell me this before?" Luc said, annoyance in his tone.

"It happened before the thief stole the Crying Crocodile and killed Julio. I was trying to stay away from trouble, like you asked. Besides, I didn't know who the second speaker was until just now. I'm not the one who's been cozying up with him in the kitchen."

"Maybe Santiago is S.J.'s 'secret informant' who told the police the master criminal was a guest here now. But Julio may not have told him the person's actual identity."

"Maybe Chef Vargas knows but won't tell because he doesn't want to end up like Julio."

"He could be in real danger."

"Wait—I remembered something else. I overheard S.J. asking Guillermo about Ana, the masseuse. She's Julio's cousin. S.J. was trying to find out how she could contact Ana."

"You sure overhear a lot of conversations. Did Guillermo tell S.J. where to find her?"

"No. He said Ana had disappeared."

CHAPTER 47

By the time cocktail hour rolled around, Iris and Luc remained secluded in their casita, unpacking a few items they'd need for one more night. They intended to ask Officer Diaz at dinner if they were allowed to leave. American Airlines had an early afternoon flight going out the next day and they hoped to be on it.

Iris's phone chimed, and seeing the sender, she felt a stab of guilt. "Damn, I promised to get back to Kelly." She read the text. "She wants us to sit with them at dinner to compare notes."

"I guess that's okay." Luc clumsily buttoned his dress shirt, twisting around to accommodate his cast. "But let's not share anything we've learned about Ana or Santiago with them. We can't trust anyone at this point."

Iris texted back a quick

> SURE

"It's not like Kelly's going to whip out a switchblade on us if *she's* the mastermind."

"At least not in front of the cop," Luc said. "Besides, according to *The Tico Times*, Julio was killed with a gun."

Iris made several passes with a mascara wand before calling out from the bathroom, "How could any of the guests have gotten a gun through airport security?"

"For what it's worth, S.J.'s profiler said the mastermind would have local accomplices. They probably did the actual robbery and murder."

"Then why would the mastermind even need to be here? I assume this person wasn't around when the other three artifacts were stolen. Why risk showing up now?"

"I'll guess shooting Julio was not in the script. But if this mastermind joined our surfing session last Saturday, they had planned all along to arrive after the first three thefts. Maybe the plan was to bump off the accomplices after the last urn was safely on its way to the U.S., to get rid of anyone who might talk."

Iris pulled a dress over her head as she mulled over this idea. "I wonder how the Big boss communicates with the accomplices. And how he or she gets around. The only guests who have a rental car are Lisa and Kelly. Come to think of it, they arrived in Costa Rica before the session began and said they had driven across the country. But what if they've been in this area the whole month, orchestrating these thefts? They speak Spanish too, so they can move around and communicate more easily than the rest of this group."

"We don't know which other guests speak Spanish. And the accomplices might speak English." Luc slipped on his espadrilles. "You ready? And remember, even if Kelly and Lisa want to play Sleuth, we should act like we're out of the game."

"*Are* we out of the game? We might need to stay in for self-preservation."

As soon as they entered the pavilion, Iris and Luc noticed Mark Harris, the resort's lawyer, sitting at a table with Lieutenant Alvarez, Cal, and Sierra. He was flipping through several pages of a document. He handed the papers back to Alvarez, and frowning, shrugged at Cal.

Kelly waved Iris and Luc over to join Lisa and her at the bar. As they approached, Kelly touched Iris's arm. "I am so sorry that we ever contacted S.J. We figured she would study the case from her studio in Chicago, not come down here and embarrass us all by implying we were suspects. I hope you're not mad."

Iris tried to rein in her annoyance at the young woman's naïveté. "I think the OIJ had reasons other than the podcast to focus on the resort guests. But it would have been nice not to have our pasts put under a microscope in front of thousands of listeners."

Kelly cringed. "Thank God S.J. didn't use people's names or call out which resort we're staying at."

Lisa quickly changed the subject. "Why do you think the lieutenant is back? And who's the other man with Cal and Sierra?"

"That's the resort's attorney," Luc explained. "And him being here can't be a good sign. I wonder if something new has happened."

Iris noticed that all the guests had now arrived and were eyeing Alvarez warily. Even Chef Vargas stood by his kitchen door, watching the officer. The soft ambient music in the room suddenly fell silent.

"I think Cal's going to make an announcement," Kelly whispered.

Cal stood up by his table, his face an expressionless mask. "I need to inform you all that Lieutenant Alvarez has an official warrant to search the casitas and the resort grounds. While the resort's attorney, Mark Harris, can't act as your personal attorney due to a possible conflict of interest, he has reviewed the warrant to make sure that it's in order. I apologize in advance for any invasion of your privacy. To minimize the disruption, the OIJ officers will carry out the search of your casitas now during cocktails and dinner. The police will not be interrogating any of you at this time. Thank you for your patience." He exchanged a worried glance with Sierra and sat down.

The noise level in the room increased as the couples expressed loud protests. Margo's voice rose above the others. "This is an outrage! I want my attorney. Some vacation this is turning out to be!" She glared at Kenneth, who in turn glared at Alvarez.

Iris couldn't disagree with Margo. She asked Luc, "Can they do this? Go through our things when we had nothing to do with the crime?"

"I don't know. Maybe we need to call Sterling. Or the American Embassy."

"But wouldn't the resort's attorney warn us if we needed to protest having them go through our stuff?" Lisa asked.

"Harris is the resort's lawyer, not ours," Luc said. "Our interests may not be the same."

"I hope the search doesn't turn up anything," Kelly said. "Then maybe they'll leave us alone."

Iris noted that Kelly and Lisa did not seem overly worried by this development. She glanced around the room. The other two couples displayed varying degrees of outrage, as well as definite nervousness. Did that imply guilt?

Sammy appeared next to their party and offered them iced mojitos on a tray. Sierra must have signaled him to keep the alcohol flowing. The music resumed playing as Tia and Eric joined their group.

"Is this turning into the Vacation from Hell, or what?" Tia said. "Is Alvarez going to apply thumbscrews to us next?"

"I didn't notice a room search clause in the brochure," Iris said.

Eric sidled over to Luc. "So, one of us stole some old urns because our restaurants need tons of cash?" He smirked. "Come on. You can confess to me."

Luc raised an eyebrow. "I'm not the one who expanded to a second restaurant and had the city stop the work. The meter's running. Gotta be nerve-racking, man." Luc slapped Eric smartly on the shoulder.

The air was thick with tension as the guests retreated to their tables for dinner. Lieutenant Alvarez left the pavilion, but Mark Harris stayed and sat, his posture rigid, with Cal and Sierra. Officer Diaz stood at the main door, arms crossed, and feet planted, as if he would tackle anyone trying to leave.

Iris tried to lighten the mood by asking Kelly and Lisa more about their drive across Costa Rica before their arrival at the resort. The women replied with stories about their adventure-packed week. The description of their road trip sounded more plausible than the idea of them hunkered down somewhere in the area arranging robberies. Iris couldn't imagine the mother and daughter as suspects unless they were both gifted actresses.

As dinner progressed, the two couples exchanged stories about other travel experiences. Inspired by the Duvals's anecdotes, Iris added the Atacama Desert in Chile and the Sossusvlei Dunes in Namibia to her travel wish list. And Luc was finally able to learn how the Duval Vineyard got started.

Iris had almost buried her annoyance about the search when Lieutenant Alvarez re-entered the pavilion. All conversations quieted, then stopped as he approached the head table and murmured something to Sierra and Cal. Sierra's fair skin turned alabaster, and a vein throbbed in Cal's temple. The couple leaned in to consult with their attorney while Alvarez stood a few feet away. Mark Harris conferred with the lieutenant before nodding and taking his seat again.

Every eye in the room was on the Senior OIJ Officer as he spoke. "I need to inform you we've discovered an object on the resort grounds which might be a critical piece of evidence."

Alvarez waited for the startled reactions to die down. "Because of this development, we need to take everyone's fingerprints. In addition, an officer will escort you to your casita tonight so you can turn over your passports. None of you may leave the resort until we can eliminate you from our suspect list."

Or eliminate most of us.

Mark Harris rose again from his seat, his hands up in a stop position. "I know this feels invasive, folks. I've read the warrant, and the judge included a provision for fingerprinting and temporary passport retention if any critical evidence was found. Please understand that this is a murder investigation and there's evidence that the perpetrator may be here at this resort. I'm afraid we need to let the officers do their jobs."

CHAPTER 48

Iris looked anxiously around the table at the three others. "They found evidence that the murderer is one of us? And they're taking away our passports? This doesn't seem real." Her stomach churned with anger at being associated with a murderer. Her eyes scanned the other two guest tables. Eric and Tia sat quietly, seemingly processing what was happening, while Margo was waving her hands and complaining loudly to Kenneth.

Kelly leaned forward. "What do you think they discovered? Was it the Crying Crocodile?"

Her mother shook her head. "I doubt it. That's probably long gone."

"I wonder how they could have searched the whole place so quickly. Was this piece of evidence buried?" Iris asked.

Conversation stopped as the wait staff circulated to fill coffee cups.

As soon as the server left, Luc said, "I agree with Lisa that the artifacts would have disappeared by now. I'll bet it's a gun."

They stared at him as they thought about his guess.

"But if it was the gun that killed Julio, why would it be here?" Iris asked. "If some accomplice stole the urn and killed Julio, wouldn't he hide the weapon in the village or out in the jungle?"

"What if the gun belongs to the mastermind who planned to use it later to kill off the accomplices?" Luc said.

"Didn't we decide that none of us guests could ever get a gun through airport security?" Iris asked. "Or wait—can you bring in an unloaded gun in your checked luggage?"

Kelly held up her phone. "Let me ask Google the regulations for Costa Rica." She thumbed in the question and read out the response. "You need to be a permanent resident of the country in order to import a gun. I guess that leaves out all the guests unless someone has a secret residency."

Luc tilted his head. "What if the accomplice bought it on the black market and passed it on after the robbery and murder to his boss?"

"The accomplice would have to be pretty trusting," Lisa said. "Or stupid."

One of the OIJ officers had set up a fingerprinting station at an empty table and Officer Diaz was leading Eric and Tia toward it. Iris could see sweat stains on Eric's shirt.

"Should we go along with this?" Iris asked Luc. "I feel like we should check with our own lawyer first."

"Try texting Sterling," Luc suggested. "See if he can give us some quick legal advice."

Iris sent her brother a message, trying to describe the crazy situation they were in now. Seconds crawled by, but her phone remained silent. In any case, they were in a jurisdiction outside his expertise.

Eric and Tia returned to their table and sank down in their seats, scrubbing their index fingers with tiny alcohol wipes provided by the policeman. Diaz now stood next to Kenneth's and Margo's table. Iris expected them to refuse to co-operate and to sit tight, but Margo stood, throwing down her napkin in disgust. Kenneth followed, brows knitted.

While they waited for their own turn, Iris asked Kelly in a low voice, "Did you ever show the officers that shard of pottery you found?"

The young woman shook her head. "Do you think I should give it to them now? They already searched the hut and didn't find anything."

"You might as well," Iris said. "Let them figure out if it's relevant or not."

Lisa hunched her shoulders and glanced around the room. "Do you think we're safe here?"

"From the murderer, the police, or the media?" Iris asked. "Until the police catch this criminal, any of them could cause us a world of harm."

CHAPTER 49

SJM

I'm at Samantha's now. She invited her daughter and son-in-law, the cop, to dinner. She didn't tell Raf why I was here, but casually asked him how the investigation was going. Thank God he's chatty and indiscreet. He heard the OIJ found a gun at the resort hidden under the yoga platform.

DC

So, they found the murder weapon! And wow—you actually saw the location, right?

Pure gold for the next episode.

SJM

I know! Evidently, the platform was moved to the beach on New Year's Eve, last Tuesday, so the gun must have been hidden after the deck was dragged back on Wednesday morning. The OIJ then fingerprinted the eight suspects, but I'd be surprised if any of them have a record. There might be fingerprints on the gun though.

DC

If only. Who do you think it is?

SJM

Jury's still out. But we're closing in. I can feel it.

DC

Great. And I found some background stuff. There were two maybe-related robberies from last year in Mexico.

In January, three gold Pre-Columbian figurines, worth about a million all together, were stolen from a Convent outside of Mazatlán.

SJM

Wait. That's on the Pacific side?

DC

Correct. Inland from Cabo. A boat ride away.

SJM

Kenneth admitted to vacationing in Cabo. But the L.A. duo could also zip down there easily. Hell, any of them could. Go on. You said two robberies.

DC

The second hit was in July from a private collection in Sinaloa, the next town over from Mazatlán.

The thief disarmed the security system and grabbed four pre-Columbian masks with embedded jewels. Valued together at $2 million.

Broke in through a side window while the owners were away. Interpol and the ICE have been trying to track down this ring but keep running into dead ends.

SJM

Dev, was that a pun?

DC

Actually, no. Zero deaths so far with the Mexican robberies.

I attached the articles from The El País English.

SJM

But why move their team to Costa Rica? Too much heat from the pursuers?

DC

Don't know. You think those robberies are related to our Animal Quartet?

SJM

Maybe. The stolen objects sound similar. Though hard to believe that one of those resort guests is capable of pulling off three heists without getting caught. None of them struck me as all that smart.

I'm still trying to find Ana, Julio's cousin. Raf says the cops can't locate her.

Samantha's going to drive me around to see the four villages tomorrow. If I can find Ana and get her to talk, we might have this series wrapped up in record time.

CHAPTER 50

Unfrickinbelievable! Now, the local-yokel cops found my gun! I can't underestimate these guys.

Why did I agree to work with amateurs this time? True, they approached me just when Interpol was turning up the heat on my original Mexican team. I certainly won't be leaving any of these jokers behind to talk. As if I'd really get them green cards. But how am I supposed to deal with them without my Beretta?

And the podcaster! What a clusterfuck! I checked on her. This Sara Jane McClinnock usually focuses on safe, flashy cold cases. Why did she decide to interfere in this active investigation? She reported the cops found the guard's phone. Where is she getting her information from? The last thing I need is more people digging into the backgrounds of the guests. Not that I have anything on the record personally that might show up. I think I've been careful about any communicating while down here. And the hut was completely cleared out.

But how can I be sure my helpers have been sufficiently scrupulous? I wish I could get rid of them, but there's too much scrutiny right now.

Plus, I need a new weapon.

CHAPTER 51

Iris slept fitfully, with images of Julio's bloodied body sprawled on the museum floor invading her dreams. When she awoke, the room was already bright. She glanced at the bedside clock and groaned. Eight-thirty, well after her usual time to rise. Luc was sitting up on his side of the bed, facing the window. He turned toward her. "You were having nightmares, babe."

"Sorry, did I wake you?"

"It's okay. I couldn't sleep much either." His hair was damp from a shower, and he was already dressed in a T-shirt and shorts.

"Let me get ready," she said.

As she sat up, Luc reached for her hand. "We should get out of here. This resort feels like a prison now, and I'm worried about the Boston press getting wind of our involvement in this mess. We could be safe at home."

"Should I try getting through to Sterling again? Maybe he can get them to release our passports. It's not even seven back in Boston, but he's an early riser. I can catch him before he heads into the office." She grabbed her phone from the nightstand and speed-dialed her brother's cell phone.

As soon as Iris heard Sterling's six-hundred-dollar-an-hour attorney voice on the line, she said a brief hello and launched into a precise description of their current predicament. When she finished, she heard his aggrieved sigh. "I'll have my paralegal, Marissa, look up the laws governing Costa Rica's ability to curtail travel of U.S. citizens who haven't been arrested for anything." There was a pause. "You haven't been arrested, right?"

"Right." Iris gritted her teeth. Sterling always expected the worst of her. Just because of those few complicated instances over the years.

"See if you can send me a copy of the warrant. Either Marissa or I will get back to you as soon as we can."

The line went dead. No words of concern, as usual. Such a sympathetic brother. At least he was offering legal input.

"He's going to get back to us once he's done some research on Costa Rica's laws." Iris rolled out of bed and headed toward the bathroom.

"Sounds like we won't have enough time before we hear back to retrieve our passports and catch that afternoon flight," Luc called to her. "I might as well go to the hospital for my appointment to get my arm checked. The doctor wants to take x-rays."

"Will Alvarez let you leave the resort grounds before we receive our 'get out of jail' documents from Sterling? And how will you get there?"

"Cal said he'd drive me after breakfast. I guess he'll be my chaperone in case I make a run for it."

"I can go with you." Iris said. "We can make a run for it together."

"No, get out there and ride some waves before we leave. I won't be gone long."

As soon as Iris and Luc entered the pavilion, Kelly got up from her table and joined them. "When I didn't see you earlier, I was afraid you guys had slipped away in the night."

"No, sorry, I overslept," Iris explained. "Are you heading out to surf now?"

"In a few minutes. Mom's gone back to the casita to put on her sunblock." Kelly looked around at the only remaining diner, Eric, reading something on his phone. She lowered her voice. "I gave Lieutenant Alvarez the pottery shard last night. He scolded me for withholding something that might be important to the case. I pointed out that I had no way of knowing that at the time." Kelly shrugged. "Anyway, he's got it now." She turned toward the door and gave them a wave. "See you at the beach."

In the back of Iris' sleep-deprived mind, she felt like there was something significant about that pottery shard, if she could only remember what.

CHAPTER 52

Iris and Luc were the only ones still sitting in the pavilion finishing their breakfast when Cal swept into the room, looking strained.

"We should get going, Luc, if we're going to make it to your ten o'clock appointment. Are you ready to go?"

"All set." Luc stood and turned to Iris, "Go take some long rides for me."

Iris followed them out into the humid heat, then headed for the beach. She found Guillermo giving the other guests a lesson about how to do a top turn on a wave. He was describing how to rotate your body weight while looking in the direction you wanted to be in to slide down the wave. He tried simultaneously to demonstrate these motions on land. Where was Mateo, his assistant?

Iris sidled up next to Tia and whispered, "Can you give me the Cliffs notes version of this?"

Tia shrugged, "Sorry, I haven't really been listening. Ask Kelly. She seems to be riveted."

Iris noticed an edge to Tia's voice, and she was tugging on her locs. "You okay?" Iris asked.

"Define okay."

Seemed like a private chat was in order. Iris nodded with her head toward the other end of the beach. "Want to play hooky and take a walk?"

"To the forbidden beach? You got it." Tia grabbed her daypack from the sand.

They backed away slowly from the group, hoping to be inconspicuous.

As they scrambled over the rocks of the promontory, they ignored Eric's plaintive shout. "Hey, where are you going?"

When they reached the other side, they took off their water sandals and stuffed them in their packs.

"Are you sure the jaguar isn't going to attack us?" Tia asked.

"They're supposed to sleep during the day, but let's walk close to the water. I'm not sure they like the salt water."

Tia raised an eyebrow. "You're betting our lives on this guess? Oh, what the hell. Let's live dangerously."

The women walked for fifteen minutes, casting occasional glances toward the jungle to see if any shiny eyes were reflected back at them.

Tia finally broke the silence. "Is it hotter today or am I just feeling grouchy about everything?"

"Grouchy? After we've been told we can't leave because we're suspects in a murder-robbery? After the police have confiscated our passports? Grouchy seems merited Iris collapsed onto the sand. "Let's sit here. I've got some sodas. They won't be cold, but better than nothing." She rummaged in her pack and produced two cans. "Red can or green can?"

Tia reached for the red. "I'll admit, I am pretty freaked out. Aren't you?"

Iris cracked the pull tab and took a sip of her soda. "I feel so bad about Julio, who I'd talked with a little. Did you know he wanted to become an architect? Sweet guy. I also feel sad for these villagers losing parts of their cultural heritage. But the crimes became personal after the police found evidence last night at the resort. I guess I never believed the mastermind was one of us. Do you think they found a gun?"

"That's what I figure. If it was serious enough to justify fingerprinting us all and taking our passports, it would have to be a weapon or one of the actual artifacts. And I suspect the urns have all left the country by now."

"I doubt that fingerprinting us will turn up anything. A criminal this smart wouldn't forget to wear gloves."

There was a pregnant pause, and Tia ran her finger around the wet top of her soda can.

"Tia?" Iris looked at her closely. "What are you not saying?"

Tia's eyes got big. "No! I'm not the one behind this business here. It's just that…well…my fingerprints may connect back to something from when I was a kid."

"Yeah, okay. Is it relevant to what's going on here?"

"Not at all. I was in high school, and a few friends and I decided to liberate some dogs from their cages at a testing lab. We got caught, and the judge sentenced us to community service. But the cops had us fingerprinted, of course. The record will probably show up in a background check."

"Personally, I think you should get a medal for trying to help those poor dogs. And I doubt something like that is going to raise any red flags." Iris gave her a half-smile. "Maybe if the Crying Crocodile was a live creature…"

Tia rolled her eyes. "I don't want that bitch, S.J. to blast my past all over her podcast. Of course, it would be the only Black guest who would have a record, right?"

"How is that woman finding out all this stuff about us? I can't believe our whole lives are out there on the internet." She looked over at Tia. "You know, you can probably get your juvenile record sealed. Do you know a lawyer who could do it right away?"

"That's a good idea. I'll call a friend I know. Maybe I can get out ahead of S.J." Tia finished her last sip of soda, stowed the empty can in her pack, and stood. "Let's keep walking. It feels good to get some exercise."

Iris held up a finger. "Hang on a second." She took out her phone and searched her messages. Nothing yet from Sterling or his paralegal. Damn. That probably meant spending yet another night at the resort, pretty much under house arrest.

CHAPTER 53

Iris and Tia continued walking for another fifteen minutes.

"Can we rest?" Tia asked. "I'm getting a stitch in my side. You'd think that after surfing for hours every day, I'd be in better shape."

"Sure, let's stop here. And we can turn back whenever you're ready. The surf lesson should be finished by the time we get there."

They plopped down onto the beach and watched the waves crashing against the shoreline. Iris kicked off her water sandals and dug her toes into the sand. The backdrop of chattering monkeys got louder and more frantic. Then the jungle became eerily quiet.

Tia sat up straight. "You smell smoke?"

Iris sniffed the air. "Maybe they're grilling lunch at the resort?"

Tia stood and looked toward the jungle. "Over there. Something's on fire!"

Iris turned to follow her gaze. A plume of gray smoke rose above the tree line. "Oh, shit!" She scrambled to her feet.

They hurried across the sand to get a closer look.

Standing at the edge of the dense jungle, Iris looked for the source of the smoke. She could make out a tan structure through the trees. "That must be the hut Luc saw. Why is it burning?" She took a step forward.

"Wait," Tia reached for Iris's arm. "The jaguar may be in there."

Then they heard a woman's scream rise above the crackling of the fire. The smoke was becoming thicker.

"Someone's trapped inside!" Iris shouted. "Call for help. I'll go see."

"Call who?"

"Try 9-1-1," Iris yelled over her shoulder. "See if that works here."

Iris moved quickly through the tangled vegetation. She could hear Tia behind her speaking breathlessly in Spanish to someone on her phone.

By the time Iris reached the hut, Tia had caught up with her. "9-1-1 got through. They're sending a helicopter."

"That'll be too late. We've got to get that woman out of there now."

Through the smoke, Iris could see a padlocked door. She got a towel out of her daypack and wrapped it around her hand. She pulled on the padlock, but it held tight. It looked new and not yet rusted in the salt air. "Hang on. We're coming in to get you," she shouted. "Stay low and cover your mouth."

Tia shouted Iris's words in Spanish.

The fire seemed to have started on the thatched roof. If the hut was constructed like the casitas, hurricane straps would connect the roof to the walls preventing her from pulling apart an opening at the eave. Iris circled the hut, looking for another way in. There were no windows. When she reached the door again, she noticed that the hinges were on the outside. She asked Tia, "Do you have a screwdriver in your pack? Or anything like a nail file?"

"Are you kidding?"

"Empty your pack on the ground."

Iris did the same. She surveyed all the contents, finding nothing that seemed useful and wondering if the edge of an empty soda can might work. Then she remembered the coins in her pack's side pocket, change from buying ice cream in the village, and shook them out onto the ground. Several coins were thin enough to fit in the screws fastening the hinges. She handed one to Tia. "You take the lower hinge. I'll take the upper." She showed her how to fit the coin edge in the screw's slot and turn it counterclockwise.

All they could hear from inside the hut was the crackling of the fire.

"Are you okay? We're trying to take the door off." Iris shouted.

They heard a low moan. It sounded like a man's voice.

"This screw is stuck." Tia swore.

"Use a bigger coin for leverage." Iris instructed.

Orange flames and towering black smoke fully engulfed the roof now. Thick fumes filled Iris's nostrils, and she tasted grit in the back of her throat.

After the upper hinge dropped from the door to the ground, Iris helped Tia work on the bottom one. When they had disconnected both hinges, the door fell awkwardly open, hanging on its padlock. Through the acrid haze of smoke, Iris got a glimpse inside to a dark space. She could barely make out a huddle of motionless figures on the ground. How many were in there?

Iris soaked her towel with some water from her bottle, and Tia followed her lead. They wrapped the wet towels around their mouths and plunged inside.

CHAPTER 54

Iris could hardly see through the smoke, but the shaft of hazy light from the open door illuminated three bodies sprawled on the ground. Moving in further, she could make out two women and one man. She grabbed the legs of the closest woman and dragged her toward the entrance. Overhead, balls of flaming thatch cascaded around them. Tia stamped out one that had landed on the second woman's sleeve and caught it on fire. Tia grabbed the woman's arm and leg and pulled her outside.

They lay the two women on the path a few faltering steps from the hut. Iris quickly registered that the women were Mateo's twin sisters. They didn't appear to be breathing. Should she and Tia stop and try to resuscitate them?

There was a strange buzzing in the air, like white noise, creating an aural curtain. The fire was moving fast. "We've got to get that guy out of there. You take his legs, I'll take his arms," Iris yelled to Tia, who nodded back. By now, flames were shivering up the walls, and the heat inside was intense. Iris could now see that the man lying on the ground was Mateo. They tried to lift him up a few inches but, despite being short, he was heavy. Iris shifted around to grab one of his legs while Tia took the other. They managed to drag him on his back as far as the doorway, just as a load of hot ash and a beam from the roof collapsed above them. The lintel above the door stopped the falling board, missing their heads by inches. They pulled Mateo out onto the path next to his sisters.

Tia ran to the beach to see if any rescue team was in sight yet. Her face was smeared with soot and Iris knew that her own must look the same.

Iris unwound the wet towel from her mouth, took a shallow breath, and immediately coughed from the smoke that still swirled around her. She took a swig from her water bottle and looked down at the motionless bodies of Mateo and his sisters. They needed CPR immediately.

Iris thought back to Kelly giving CPR to Luc. She stretched out Violetta on her back, cleared her mouth and, interlocking her hands, started chest compressions. How many was she supposed to do? A lot, she thought, so she counted out twenty-four. Violetta was still not breathing. Iris put her mouth over the woman's and breathed hard several times, trying to ignore the taste of smoke and spit. She squatted back to study Violetta's face for some sign of life.

Where was Tia? "Come help me!" Iris shouted toward the beach.

Tia crashed back through the vegetation. "I don't see anyone coming."

"Give the other woman CPR," Iris ordered. "Clasp your hands together like this and press quickly two dozen times." She returned to trying to revive Violetta. After Iris had completed another round, she saw Violetta's chest start to rise spasmodically. The woman let out a slight whimper and rolled over to her side.

Iris glanced at Tia as she moved over to work on Mateo. The name Veronica popped into her head. That was the other twin. Iris's gaze shifted slightly and became mesmerized by two intense golden eyes staring at her from behind a tree twenty feet away. She imagined she could hear a chorus of soft growls. The jaguar was awake!

"Don't move, Tia."

Tia slowly lifted her head and spotted the predator. "Shit. What do we do?"

"Back up *very* slowly."

As they were carefully rising from their crouches, a loud chuff-chuffing filled the air. The sound of rotor blades intensified as a helicopter flew into sight above them. Iris looked back for the jaguar. It was gone. She let out her breath. The cavalry had arrived!

A loud, distorted voice came from the helicopter loudspeaker: "Please move yourselves and the bodies away from the fire. Retreat to the beach. We are going to drop powder on the flames." The voice repeated the message in Spanish.

Iris could see that the fire had spread to the nearby trees. She and Tia exchanged exhausted looks. They lifted Veronica between them, propping her arms around their shoulders. The woman's head hung down, and it was hard to tell if she was breathing. They dragged her to the sand and went back for Violetta. After hauling both sisters to safety, they stumbled back for Mateo. But all they found was an empty depression where his body had been. Drag marks led into the dense underbrush under branches too low for any human to pass under.

Iris hesitated. Should she try to go after him? She'd never be able to wrestle him away from a jaguar, assuming he was even still alive.

"Leave the area immediately!"

The message from the loudspeaker made her options clear. She and Tia scurried to the beach just before a cloud of bright red powder from the plane blanketed the flames.

CHAPTER 55

As they waited on the beach, Iris continued to give Veronica CPR. Tia felt the woman's wrist for a pulse before saying, "I think she's gone."

Iris checked on Violetta, who was curled into a fetal position on the sand, her hand twitching slightly. At least she seemed to be alive.

The percussive thwapping from the helicopter grew louder as it approached. It hovered forty feet away from them, then descended slowly to land on the beach. Iris and Tia covered their ears and squeezed their eyes shut from the flurry of sand.

With the engine still running, two men jumped out of the rear of the aircraft and shook open a collapsible stretcher. A petite woman in a black police uniform climbed out of the front seat. Iris and Tia directed the EMTs to Violetta and tried to explain over the noise of the engine about their attempts to resuscitate both women. After trying to find Veronica's pulse, one EMT gave the other a subtle head shake, but they fitted oxygen masks on both sisters and ferried them to the helicopter in shifts. Then the EMTs returned to check on Iris and Tia.

Between breaths through their own oxygen masks, Iris and Tia received treatment for some small first-degree burns on their hands. After applying salves to their wounds, the EMTs took off in the helicopter to get Violetta and her unfortunate sister to a hospital.

The police officer, who identified herself as Isobel Lopez, remained on the beach and asked Iris and Tia about their discovery of the fire at the hut and its victims. The two women described the events and explained how it looked like a jaguar had dragged Mateo's body into the jungle. Iris walked Officer Lopez over to the spot where she had last seen him. The officer rapidly thumbed notes on her phone and took photos. She retrieved a red flag from her pocket and poked it into the earth where Mateo had lain. "A full forensic team will arrive soon to examine this site," she assured them.

Iris was beyond exhausted. She wished there had been space to hitch a ride in the helicopter as she contemplated the long walk back to the resort. She looked over at Tia. "You okay?"

"Worst vacation ever!" Tia muttered. The whites of her eyes stood out against the grime covering her face.

Officer Lopez handed them bottles of water. "Do you have enough energy to walk with me back to the resort?" she asked.

"What are our other options?" Tia asked.

"I could radio in to get other officers down here to help you walk."

There was clearly not going to be an ATV or a boat ride on offer, so Iris said, "We can make it if we walk slowly, right?"

Tia nodded unenthusiastically.

With their flagging energy, the trip back took a long forty minutes in the hot sun. Plenty of time for Iris to wonder who had trapped Mateo and his sisters in the hut before setting that deadly fire, and why.

CHAPTER 56

My plan was ingenious. Mateo agreed to meet me in the hut with his sisters so I could photograph them for their new passports and visas. We would discuss arrangements to get them to the States, get them jobs, and a place to live. They were so excited they didn't notice when I slipped out and snapped on the padlock. I lit up the washcloth I brought and tossed it up onto the roof. They didn't start screaming until I was thirty feet away, admiring the flames.

But who would hear them out there, miles from the resort? Someone would eventually notice the smoke, but the three of them would be toast by then. Burnt toast. It's not as if anyone walks on this beach in the middle of the morning.

Except this morning. Except friggin' Iris, the architect, and that bitch, Tia. I barely slipped by them along the edge of the jungle while they were sitting there, staring out at the ocean. I figured the smoke would have knocked out my ex-helpers by the time those two got close to the hut.

But were Mateo and his sisters really dead? I saw a helicopter zip over there. Was that to put out the fire or to rescue still-breathing bodies?

I need to assume the worst. I haven't gotten this far by failing to cover my tracks. All it would take would be for one of my ex-helpers to still be conscious enough to croak out my name.

I need to make sure the whole lot of them are dead, then get the hell out of Dodge. But how do I get my passport back?

CHAPTER 57

When Iris, Tia, and Officer Lopez finally arrived back at the resort around one o'clock, the beach was empty. Before they headed inside the buildings, Lopez cautioned them. "It's vital you don't mention whether Mateo or his sisters survived the fire. In fact, say as little as possible about what you saw back there this morning. There's a dangerous killer on the loose, and you can best stay safe by acting as if you know little about what's going on."

Tia shot Iris a skeptical look. "I think our fellow guests know us better than that."

"You'd better hope not," Lopez retorted. "Please help us keep things quiet for now."

On the long walk back, Iris had concluded that the three siblings must have been accomplices of the robbery mastermind, and he or she wanted them dead to ensure their silence. It would also save having to pay them a share of the profits from the sale of the urns.

Given the impressive quality of Veronica's computer at the orphanage, she must have been the one who remotely disconnected the museums' security systems. If the pottery shard that Kelly had found near the hut had come from one of Violetta's enormous pots, maybe the artifacts were hidden inside them before being smuggled out on the midnight cigarette boat.

Did that mean that Mateo had shot Julio? The two men were from the same village and had worked together at the resort. If Mateo had actually pulled the trigger, that would make him a cold-blooded monster, or at least a desperate man. And now he was dead.

But that left the bigger question of who the mastermind was. Julio's last text to Ana implied it was one of the resort guests. That guest had somehow lured Mateo and his sisters to the hut this morning. Everyone but Luc and Margo were at the surf lesson when Iris had arrived, weren't they? She tried to picture the scene. Had Kenneth been there?

Or maybe someone had trapped the siblings earlier, and the fire had started slowly. She and Luc had been the last ones to leave breakfast. Could someone have imprisoned them, then snuck back in time for the surf lesson? Kelly took a long run on that beach each morning before breakfast. And why was Eric so concerned when he saw Iris and Tia heading off in the direction of the hut?

But if the fire was set while she and Tia were walking down the beach, how did they miss seeing anyone returning to the resort? The jungle was too dense to traverse and there were no paths as far as she knew. Did the killer slip behind them while they were resting, looking out at the waves? Iris felt goosebumps creeping up her arms.

Officer Lopez' lapel speaker squawked something unintelligible in Spanish, and she pressed a button on top of the unit to respond. She turned to the women. "The rest of the guests are eating lunch in the pavilion now. You are welcome to join them. But after lunch, Lieutenant Alvarez wants you to meet with him to go over your statements about this morning."

Tia's mouth took on a mutinous set as she glared at Lopez. "If you want us to downplay our role in rescuing people trapped in a burning hut at great risk to ourselves, I suggest that Iris and I go to our casitas, take showers, and change into some presentable clothes before appearing in public."

By the time Iris had cleaned up and gotten herself over to the pavilion, the guests were lingering over their after-lunch coffees. Everyone looked curious and concerned as she came in. She had the sense they were waiting to extract details about the morning's events. They had probably smelled the fire and heard the helicopter. There must have been a lot of speculation.

Luc crossed the room and hugged Iris, then held her at arm's length. "Are you okay? We heard there was a fire down by the hut and that you and Tia were there. What happened? You should have called me!"

Iris held on to him and whispered in his ear, "I'll tell you later." She didn't need to worry about keeping the truth from Luc. *He* wasn't the mastermind. But why hadn't she thought to call him on her long walk back?

She glanced around the room to try to gauge each person's mood. Most of them were pretending not to watch her. Tia was sitting at a table with Eric, eating lunch. Iris caught her eye, but the look she returned was hard to decipher. Iris wondered what Tia might have already said before Iris arrived. They should have coordinated their stories beforehand.

Lieutenant Alvarez, seated with Officer Lopez, Siena and Cal, was watching Iris while finishing his lunch.

Iris sat down at their table and ordered the seafood paella and an iced tea from the hovering server before turning to Luc. "How was your check-up?"

"The bone's healing okay. I'll have my own doctor look at it when I get home." He reached over and examined her hands. "Are these burn marks? Were you actually at the fire? I thought you were just watching from the beach."

Iris casually covered her mouth with her hand and said, "Don't react! I'm not supposed to be telling you this. Tia and I were warned not to say anything, but someone tried to kill Mateo and his sisters by roasting them alive inside the hut."

Luc's expression remained neutral, but his eyebrows popped up. He dropped them quickly and smiled, lifting his cast as if they'd been discussing his hospital check-up. "Uh, huh. Go on."

"We broke into the hut and dragged the bodies out. Gave them CPR. I think only Violetta survived."

A muscle in Luc's jaw contracted.

The server arrived with Iris's late lunch and an espresso for Luc. After she left, Luc ran a lemon peel around the edge of his tiny cup and asked, "Where was the fire-setter while this was going on?"

"I don't know. They might have circled back to the resort along the edge of the jungle when Tia and I weren't looking."

"So, it could have been someone in this room? And they could have seen you there."

Iris glanced around, her fork paused in mid-air. "Uh, huh."

"This is not good. We've got to get out of here."

"Or else learn who the dangerous person is and let the police know." She took one more bite and tried to chew it. She had lost her appetite. "Maybe you could talk to Chef Vargas. Find out if he knows who the mastermind might be. He may open up to you. After we finish lunch, Tia and I are supposed to give Alvarez a written transcript about what happened this morning."

Iris took one more bite, then bunched up her napkin and laid it on the table. "I'd better get my statement over with. See you back in the casita afterward." She got up and reluctantly walked over to meet the lieutenant.

CHAPTER 58

SJM

You won't believe what's happened this morning! When Samantha and I were visiting the villages where the robberies occurred, we heard a helicopter landing nearby in the Nosara hospital parking lot.

We watched EMTs unload two bodies on stretchers and take them inside. Samantha worked her way over to an observer who seemed knowledgeable and learned that there'd been a fire in the jungle, down the beach from the resort.

These two women had gotten burned. The EMTs were focusing their attention on only one of the women, so I think the other may have been okay or dead.

DC

Is it two of the resort guests? Who else would be in that jungle behind the beach?

Wait—isn't that where the hut is? This could have something to do with the smuggling ring.

SJM

But two women? Not to be sexist, but what is their role? Samantha's going to call her son-in-law, the cop, and see if he can tell us anything about what's going on.

DC

Sounds like a juicy development for the next podcast. Things are moving almost too fast!

CHAPTER 59

Luc found Santiago in the kitchen scraping debris from the bottom of a pan into a food compost bucket. Two young men were quietly loading plates into the large industrial dishwasher.

Santiago looked up in surprise. "You've come to help me clean up, Luc? You must be missing your own kitchen really badly."

Luc smiled. "Another fine meal, Chef. I wouldn't mind learning what herbs you put in your paella, but that isn't why I'm here." He glanced over at the men's backs. "It won't take long, but could we talk outside in your garden?"

Santiago regarded him quizzically, then led him out the back door. Luc followed him along the garden path until Santiago stopped under the fruit trees in the far corner.

"Is this private enough?" Santiago leaned against the reed fence, arms crossed over his chest.

Luc nodded. "I don't mean to overstep, so please tell me if you'd rather not talk about what's going on at the resort. I'm sure you've heard about the fire this morning over in the jungle."

Santiago gave him a cautious nod.

"And I'm sure you know the police think someone very dangerous is staying here at the resort now, a person responsible for stealing artifacts that belong to the Costa Rican people. Someone who is also responsible for killing Julio as he was trying to protect one of the artifacts."

Santiago shoved his hands into the pockets of his pants and frowned at the ground.

"Was Julio a friend?"

"Yes," was all Santiago said.

Luc debated whether he should reveal what Iris had told him in private but didn't see much choice if he wanted to get the man to open up. "There have been more deaths. This is confidential, but someone killed Mateo and his sister this morning. They were trapped inside that hut down the beach before someone intentionally set it on fire. His other sister may have survived."

Santiago sucked in a sharp breath. "Dios Mio! Are you sure Mateo is dead?"

"That's what Iris said. She tried to save them. I don't know all the details." Seeing how shocked Santiago looked, Luc felt bad. "I'm sorry about all this."

"Are you kidding? I hated that bastard, Mateo. He killed Julio! He was in on the thefts. I couldn't risk telling this to the police and ending up like Julio. I have my family to think of. But you're sure he's dead, right?"

"That's what Iris thought. I can get you more details once I talk with her. Is it safe now for you to tell the police that Mateo shot Julio?"

Santiago paused to consider. "Not until the Big boss is caught. Whoever that is, they must have killed Mateo."

"You don't know who the Big boss is?"

"No. I only know Mateo bragged that he and his sisters were soon going to live in El Norte in a fancy apartment and have good jobs."

Santiago glanced back toward the door, and Luc knew he couldn't keep the chef away from his work much longer.

"Why was Mateo so eager to leave here? This place is paradise, and he seemed to be doing pretty well," Luc said.

Santiago gave a tiny shrug. "He visited the US on some student exchange program back when he was in high school. Mateo stayed with a family for a whole year and came back with stars in his eyes. Everyone there had a fancy car and a big house with a swimming pool.

He wanted that for himself. But it's not easy getting US residency. You need a sponsor or family there. I guess he figured helping with these robberies was the way north for himself and his sisters. But for Mateo to kill Julio when he got in his way, that was pure evil."

"And, instead, the plan ended up getting him killed. Do you know where in the States Mateo spent that year?"

"I once saw a picture of him with the American kid whose family he lived with. But I don't remember much about the setting." Santiago squinted his eyes in thought. "The other boy had on a baseball cap. It had an H over a star on it, if that helps."

It took Luc, a big baseball fan, seconds to place the logo of the Houston Astros. Texas it was.

CHAPTER 60

Iris reread her statement for Lieutenant Alvarez and was signing it when she saw Luc emerge into the pavilion through the kitchen door.

He walked over and whispered in her ear, "You okay?"

As the lieutenant collected the papers and shuffled them into his briefcase, Iris cocked her head toward the entrance. "I will be. Let's get out of here."

They said nothing more until they were inside the casita and Iris had locked the door behind her. Luc pointed toward the minibar. "Drink?"

"God, yes."

He filled two highball glasses halfway with chilled tonic water, then added a hefty pour of vodka and handed one to Iris. Slumping down in a lounge chair, he rested his drink on the arm. "Sorry, no ice or lime."

She settled in the chair facing him, gave her drink a twirl with her finger, then drained half of the glass. Checking her phone, she spotted a text from her brother.

CALL ME

was all it said. "Hey, maybe Sterling has some good news." She speed-dialed him back and put the call on speakerphone.

"Iris," Sterling answered. "Wait, am I on speakerphone? Who else is there? This is confidential information." Suspicious, as always.

"It's just Luc and I."

"Luc and me," Sterling corrected. "I had my paralegal check Costa Rican law and, technically, they can't detain you unless you've been arrested."

"So, we can leave?" Iris asked.

"Not so fast. I had Marissa review the warrant the judge signed, and it states that if any incriminating evidence is found on the resort grounds, such as a possible murder weapon, the guests and staff must remain on site where officers may question them over the next forty-eight hours. You may each retain your own lawyer."

"We're stuck here for two days?" Luc asked. "They took our passports."

"You're all considered suspects in this looting/murder case, so yes, they can detain you."

"I should probably mention that the body count has gone up since we spoke," Iris said. "A surf instructor and his two sisters were trapped inside a hut that was set on fire this morning."

"Intentionally?" Sterling asked.

"Very much so. One of the sisters may survive, but she's in the hospital and, as far as I know, hasn't said who lured them to the hut."

Sterling's voice was stern. "Please tell me you were nowhere near this hut at the time."

"A friend and I were walking on the beach, and we saw smoke. We managed to drag the bodies out and give the women CPR, but the man got dragged into the jungle by a jaguar." Iris paused. "I think he was already dead."

"Pfft. You're making this up."

"I wish I was."

Sterling sighed dramatically. "Do the police suspect you and your friend of setting this fire?"

That idea brought Iris up short. "I don't think so. We explained how we tried to save the victims. Anyway, we now think the surf instructor and his two sisters were involved in the theft ring and the mastermind was trying to kill them to make sure they didn't talk."

"This was supposed to be a vacation, Iris! Why do these things keep happening to you?"

Luc muttered something inaudible.

Iris raised her eyebrows and shot him a *you-too?* look. "Hopefully, the OIJ has some forensic evidence from the gun, or whatever they found last night, and maybe something from the fire this morning to implicate the real criminal. But whoever that person is may think the victims told us something before they died. We could be in danger."

"Hmm. I agree. I'd better find you a good local criminal attorney as soon as possible. I'll get back to you."

"Wait," Luc called out. "Do Iris and I each need our own lawyer?"

But the call had ended.

"Well, that wasn't good news." Iris turned off her phone. "We're stuck here for two days, and Sterling thinks the OIJ may find it suspicious that I've been so close to all the action."

"I'm the one who discovered the cigarette boat and the hut," Luc pointed out.

"Then I guess we must be in it together. Think we'll get adjacent jail cells?" Iris stood and flopped back onto the bed. "What are we going to do with the rest of our time here?"

"At least you can still surf, and we can count on eating well."

"That reminds me, did you find out anything from Chef Vargas?"

"Maybe." Luc filled her in on what Santiago appeared to know and why he was too scared to tell the police. "But Santiago didn't know the identity of the big boss who was pulling Mateo's strings. He guessed, by Mateo's bragging, that he and his sisters were promised US residency in exchange for their help with the museum thefts."

"But why would Mateo steal from his own people and kill a colleague just to get to the US?"

"He had been on a high-school exchange program there and had a rosy view of American life. He was grabbing at an easy way to get rich."

"Mateo was what—in his early twenties? So high school was only a few years ago. Could the big boss be someone he met during that program who contacted him later? Or, no. Mateo would have made the contact, hoping the person in the States was influential and would sponsor him and his sisters."

Iris tilted her head, contemplating. "But how does this get us any closer to figuring out who the hell the big boss is?"

Luc spread out his hands. "I forgot to tell you. Santiago once saw a photo of Mateo, standing with the boy whose family he was living with during his year abroad. The kid was wearing a Houston Astros baseball cap."

Iris sucked in a breath. "I knew it—Kenneth is the boss! S.J. had said he had some kids, and he's from Houston. He could have hosted Mateo while he was still living with his last wife. I thought the "cattle futures" job sounded pretty sketchy."

"Uh, don't forget that Margo's also from Houston, and didn't S.J. say that she had a son, too? She might be the one Mateo stayed with."

"Margo?" Iris tried to imagine her orchestrating this series of robberies in two different countries. "I suppose she could be putting on a ditsy act to deflect attention. But wait—people from California and other places wear Astros hats too. The others don't have any boys, but they could have crossed paths somewhere with Mateo. And even if he had been hosted by a family in Texas, it doesn't mean that one of those parents is the mastermind of all this."

"Let's let Alvarez figure this out. But who's going to tell him about Mateo's year in the US? Once the OIJ knows about that, they can find out who he stayed with."

"Do you think Chef Vargas will change his mind and speak with Alvarez now that Mateo is dead? He's the one who saw the photo with the kid's baseball cap."

Luc shook his head. "He says he won't say anything until the big boss is in the hands of the OIJ. He doesn't want to end up like Julio, or Mateo, or Veronica."

CHAPTER 61

SJM

Samantha's son-in-law was here at lunchtime, so I got more of the scoop about the fire. The two women were twin sisters of Mateo, the surf instructor at the resort.

The word that Raf got from his OIJ buddy is that Mateo and his sisters might have been accomplices for the master thief, who was trying to silence them.

One sister was a computer whiz, and the other was a potter (not sure how she fit in). First sister died of smoke inhalation, second sister still on life support at hospital.

Apparently, Iris Reid and maybe someone else (the boyfriend, Luc?) dragged the bodies out of a shack before they were burned. Boy, would I like to interview Iris. Do you think she'd talk to me?

DC

Ooh, major drama! Why was Iris there? I thought they were out surfing in the mornings. Seems suspicious.

> Are they sure she didn't start the fire? As for getting an interview with her: doubtful.
>
> Those guests/suspects must be pretty skittish about talking publicly now. And don't forget that one of them, at least, is a murderer.
>
> Kelly might talk, though. Text her. Isn't she tight with Iris?
>
> BTW, what happened to Mateo?

SJM

That's the best part! He was eaten by a jaguar!

> DC
>
> No frickin' way! This story gets better and better. We're going to win an Ambie award!
>
> Looted antiquities, a murdered guard, suspects staying at a fancy resort, a fire with trapped bodies, an accomplice eaten by a jaguar, twin sisters semi-burned alive…my God!
>
> What doesn't this story have? I'm thinking we sell it to Netflix as the next White Lotus!
>
> Sorry. Got carried away. What happened to the surf instructor?

SJM

Iris dragged Mateo out of the burning shack

(or maybe it was Luc. I need to confirm these details),

but while she was carrying the women away from the flames, Mateo's body disappeared.

The cops found pieces of him scattered around the jungle.

A jaguar was known to be living in that area and Iris claimed to have seen it watching her from back in the trees.

> **DC**
>
> Has the OIJ zeroed in on the mastermind of this whole operation?
>
> How many bodies do we have now? The guard, the sister, Mateo (unclear if he was killed by smoke or by the jaguar), and an attempt on the other sister.
>
> OMG, does that qualify as a serial killer?
>
> No wait. To be a serial, you need at least three killings spaced out over time.

SJM

And we don't know who killed the guard. Probably Mateo.

Why don't you dig out some photos of Mateo and his sisters?

Ideally, the sisters are cute and identical (always popular), and hopefully the surfer is ripped (find shirtless photo). The resort website should tell you his last name.

> **DC**
>
> I know the drill. Will you have the recording ready to post tomorrow?

SJM

Of course!

CHAPTER 62

Iris's hand trembled as she lifted a few sundresses out of her suitcase to hang back up in the closet. "How are we going to survive two more days trapped here with a murderer?" she said to Luc.

"One more day and change. The clock started ticking last night." With his arm still in a cast, Luc was struggling to pull on his swimming trunks. "The killer shouldn't view us as a threat. We need to lie low for twenty-eight more hours or until they capture the guy."

"I hope you're right." Iris moved closer to help him. "You going in the pool? Is it safe to be outside?"

"Alvarez said he was leaving several officers here to keep watch. I can't stay cooped up inside this casita much longer. I need some exercise."

"Maybe I'll sit out on the veranda and read. That way, if Margo makes any more creepy advances, I can hear your scream."

"LOL," Luc said, heading out the door. Iris grabbed her Kindle and followed him out. She took a seat on the veranda with her back close to the casita wall. No one was going to sneak up on her.

She dived back into the latest Mick Herron book, trying to put faces on his witty dialogue when she heard footsteps approaching along the path. Was it one of the police officers patrolling the grounds?

When she recognized Margo drawing near, Iris's first instinct was to shout out a warning to her. It was dangerous to wander around outside with a murderer on the loose. But surely Margo knew that. Iris sat bolt upright. If the woman was showing no fear for her own safety ...

A light blinked on in her brain. *Where are the police?* Margo couldn't really be the mastermind behind these crimes, could she? Had they all underestimated her?

Margo, smiling sweetly, slipped into the chair across from hers. Iris's thoughts were buzzing, but she pasted on a neutral expression.

"How are you holding up, hon?" Margo asked, her voice like corroded honey.

"I'm hanging in. How about you?" Would Margo be so bold as to attack her outside in broad daylight? Was there anything nearby she could use as a weapon?

"Eager to get home, you know, after all this drama." Margo drawled out the last word, as if to make light of the situation. "I hear you and Tia found those poor souls caught in the fire. That must have been terrifying for you."

Iris thought she caught a gleam in Margo's eyes. And then ... nothing. Over in a second. Excitement?

More terrifying for the poor souls. "Yes, it was," Iris replied. Margo seemed to be fishing for something.

"I hear it was Mateo and his sisters. Will they be okay?"

"How did you hear that?" Iris asked. Had Margo already pumped Tia for information?

"Oh, word gets around in a small group like this. It's hard to keep anything a secret."

So, she wanted to know if the poor souls had said anything to Iris or Tia. If they had mentioned who they were collaborating with, she and Tia would need to be silenced.

Iris checked her watch, got to her feet, and grabbed her phone. "I promised my attorney I'd FaceTime him now, but thanks for stopping by. You take care, Margo."

One of Margo's hands disappeared behind her back. Iris quickly glanced away, pretending not to notice. *Where are those police officers?*

Margo studied Iris, her eyes unblinking. "I hope this is the end of these tragedies." There was something flat and distant in her tone. A steeliness. A threat?

Iris stood, looking down at Margo expectantly, holding her phone at the ready for the imaginary meeting.

"I just wanted to check in on you." Margo finally stood and offered Iris a tight smile. "Make sure that you're okay after such a frightening experience. See you at dinner."

Iris waited until the woman was out of sight, then moved over to the lounge chair where she'd been sitting. She lifted the seat cushion, and something caught her eye. Something shiny wedged underneath. A gold cigarette lighter. It resembled the one Kenneth used to light his infernal cigars. She carefully replaced the cushion and hurried off to find Luc.

CHAPTER 63

Iris was relieved to find Luc standing by the pool, perfectly intact, toweling off. He jumped when she came up behind him.

"You scared me," he said.

"Sorry. We need to find the lieutenant. I just had a strange visit from Margo. She sat down across from me, uninvited, and hid Kenneth's lighter in the cushions of our veranda chair. I think she's the one who lit the fire this morning, and I suspect *she's* trying to frame *us*."

"You didn't touch the lighter, did you?"

"Of course not. I left it where she planted it."

"I think the police are still here in the management office. We need to tell them about this."

They followed the path to the closest casita to the pavilion.

Iris knocked on the door but, getting no response, tried the knob. It swung open. The light was dim when she and Luc entered. Suddenly, the door banged closed behind them. Turning, they saw Margo pointing a pistol straight at Iris's head. "I thought you might be coming here." She appeared calm. "Both of you, get down on the floor."

Where are the police? We need to stall her. Iris sat on the ground next to Luc, and they held their hands above their heads. "You'll get caught, Margo." She tried to keep the quaver out of her voice. "Don't make things worse. Lieutenant Alvarez is closing in." She hoped this was true.

Iris heard a moan coming from the corner. Officer Lopez slumped on the floor with her hands tied behind her back. The police officer seemed barely conscious. Margo must have taken the woman off guard and gotten hold of her gun.

"You and the boyfriend had a shootout with this cop, Iris. Luc took her gun and shot her. Then, realizing you were both trapped, you decided that murder-suicide was better than life in prison."

"No one's going to believe that," Iris protested. The gun was still in Margo's right hand, but it had slid from Iris to Luc, the barrel now pointing at his shoulder.

"Maybe I'll come up with something better," Margo mused, "after you're dead."

Out of the corner of her eye, Iris saw Luc edging slowly away from her. It was always a wise strategy for potential targets to increase the distance between them.

Margo tossed a set of plastic zip ties to Iris. "Tie up Luc's hands behind his back. Make it tight. Believe me, I'm going to check."

Iris's Sensei always warned that a brown belt in karate was no match for an opponent with a gun, especially one pointed so close to Luc's heart. If it were to move a tiny bit to one side, Iris might have a chance, providing she was fast enough. She'd have to be patient.

Iris collected the ties. She gave Luc a slight nod and crouched on her knees next to him, pretending to tie his hands together. Because of his cast, the ties wouldn't have fit around his wrists, anyway. Margo's forgetting that was her first mistake. They'd have to make their move before she noticed, while they both had their hands free.

Luc sat facing Margo, so their captor would have to walk around him to examine the zip-ties.

Disarming an opponent was incredibly risky, and Iris bet the Texan was a steady shot. Iris's pulse started to hammer. She took a deep, even breath in and blew it out slowly.

Margo kept her pistol pointed at Luc's shoulder as she approached. But when she began to circle around him, her hand shifted slightly outward. Iris launched herself up and across Luc's back. She shoved the gun out of Margo's hand with a hooking block, then elbowed her in the nose. She could feel and hear the crunch of the bone breaking.

Margo howled and reached for her bleeding face, staring at Iris in disbelief. Drops of blood spattered on the floor.

As soon as he'd sensed Iris making her move, Luc had ducked out of the way, seconds before the gun clattered to the floor. Now he grabbed it and scrambled to his feet.

Enraged, Margo lunged at Iris's throat with both hands. Iris batted them away with a reverse circle block, then grabbed Margo by the wrists and jerked them down.

"It's over, Margo." Luc said. "Down on your knees."

Seeing Luc aiming the gun squarely at her heart, Margo slowly knelt. Iris grabbed the zip-ties off the floor and bound her wrists behind her. Iris fished her phone out of her pocket and called Lieutenant Alvarez.

CHAPTER 64

Surprisingly, a few minutes later, the person who burst into the manager's office was Kelly, a shoulder holster strapped over her T-shirt, a semi-automatic pistol in front of her in a professional two-handed hold. Her eyes swept the room, taking in Officer Lopez huddled in the corner and Luc training a gun on Margo, who was on her knees with her hands behind her back.

Kelly called to Luc. "Better drop that gun before the OIJ arrives. We wouldn't want any confusion about who the bad guy is."

Luc carefully laid the gun on the floor and slid it toward Kelly. She kicked it into a distant corner, then went over to check Officer Lopez's pulse. "Hang in there, Isobel. The ambulance is coming."

Kelly checked that the restraints on Margo were secure and walked back to the doorway, now aiming her gun at the floor.

Iris closed her gaping mouth. She couldn't reconcile her image of Kelly with this woman's new air of authority. "Who *are* you?"

"I'm still Kelly Duval. Sorry, but I failed to mention our family's other career. In addition to running the vineyard, I work for Interpol like my father did as an undercover agent for the Antiquities Trafficking Unit. My father was killed last year as he was closing in on *her* criminal ring in Mexico." She gave Margo a venomous look. "We weren't sure about the identity of the ringleader and how he or she was acquiring the pieces, but Interpol got a tip that the Mexican thefts were tied to these Costa Rican ones. Guillermo reported to the OIJ last month he'd heard a rumor that the big boss of the urn thefts was scheduled to stay at this resort right about now. My mother and I felt we owed it to my father to come and make sure that this greedy piece of garbage got caught." She walked over to Margo and gave her a hard kick in the shin.

"Ow!" Margo pouted. "I want my attorney."

"I'm sure you do," Kelly growled.

Luc wrapped his unbroken arm around Iris's waist and held her tight.

There was a loud knock on the door, and Kelly backed up to open it. She spoke with the lieutenant briefly, then he entered with the OIJ officers and the EMTs. The medics quickly checked Officer Lopez' vital signs, affixed an oxygen mask over her mouth, and carried her out on a stretcher.

"Is she going to be okay?" Luc asked.

"I think so," Kelly answered. "Violetta wasn't so lucky. She died at the hospital."

The three of them looked daggers at Margo, who whined, "What about me? Am I going to get medical attention? I'm hurt."

"On your feet," Lieutenant Alvarez ordered her. Surrounded by policemen in uniforms, she was marched out of the room.

Before Kelly could follow, Iris touched her arm. "What about Kenneth? Was he in on Margo's plans?"

"I wondered about that," Kelly admitted. "We actually suspected Kenneth or Eric of being the big boss. Sexist, I know. We weren't sure if Mateo was involved, but Chef Vargas told us last night about his foreign exchange year as a student in the US, and the photo with the Astros baseball cap. That let us trace his stay to Margo's family. After we focused in on her art gallery, we were able to work backwards to discover how the operation worked. Margo had local criminals in Mexico stealing artifacts and hiding them in crates of pottery to slip through customs. We haven't found any links to Kenneth, and it looks so far like he was an unknowing dupe she used as camouflage."

"Ouch. I almost feel sorry for the guy," Luc said.

"Don't," Kelly responded. "He's basically a grifter and into some deep trouble with loan sharks. The FBI will keep their eye on him."

"How about Lisa? Didn't she want to be here to see Margo apprehended?" Iris asked.

"Mom's out by herself walking on the beach. She didn't trust herself to be in the same room with the woman responsible for killing Dad."

Iris squeezed her hand. "I'm sorry about that."

Kelly smiled sadly and turned away, leaving Iris and Luc alone in the manager's office.

"You know, you had me a little nervous back there with the gun," Luc said. "I'm glad I interpreted your look to duck correctly."

"And I'm glad my reflexes are still fast."

"How confident were you that you could push Margo's trigger hand out of the way in time?"

"Completely," she lied.

CHAPTER 65

SJM

Hold the presses! (I always wanted to say that.) It's friggin' Margo! She's the mastermind! Raf swung by Samantha's condo after work and filled us in. They caught her!

DC

Seriously? Margo? How did they figure it out? Are they sure?

SJM

Raf said the OIJ had been coordinating all along with an undercover Interpol agent—guess who that is!

Background searches turned up that Mateo had stayed with Margo's family in Houston during high school, on a foreign exchange program.

Once they had that connection, they dug into her art gallery records and found some interesting ties to the Mexican thefts.

DC

How did we miss that? I did our regular background searches on all the guests. So Mateo was the accomplice like you thought.

Now come on—who's the Interpol agent? One of the guests?

Wait—I bet it's Cal. You said he has a scar on his face. That tracks.

SJM

No, I figure the agent is Iris, but Interpol keeps their undercover agents' identities super-secret.

We should keep an eye on her in the future. She gets mixed up in a lot of dicey stuff back at home.

DC

What about Kenneth? Was he involved? He must have suspected something.

SJM

OIJ doesn't think so, but they're holding him until they're sure. He struck me as the perfect dupe—too self-centered to notice much outside his own little world.

Margo's way smarter than I gave her credit for. And dangerous. She shot a local cop when she was cornered. Didn't kill her, but still.

DC

Yikes! So, what happens now? Obviously, you'll update the podcast for tomorrow.

What kind of jail sentence might Margo get? Does she stand trial in the States, Costa Rica, or Mexico—which comes first?

And are the other guests all leaving? You should talk to your friend Kelly to find out what the others are making of all this.

SJM

Contact our attorney listener, Beverley, and ask her what will happen with jurisdiction. We'll need to do follow-ups on Margo's trials and sentencing. Too bad this got resolved so quickly. I had enough material for a whole month of podcasts. And the trials will take months, or years.

DC

Not to get lost in the shuffle: did they ever find the four urns? What will happen to them?

SJM

Good question. I'll see if Raf knows. Stay tuned!

CHAPTER 66

Iris couldn't believe she and Luc voluntarily stayed on for two more days at the resort after Margo had been apprehended. The OIJ had hustled off Kenneth on Wednesday for questioning and he hadn't reappeared, while Tia and Eric had lost no time finding a flight back to L.A. But the Duvals stuck around so Kelly could tie up loose ends in the case. And Sierra convinced Iris and Luc to stay and finish their vacation now that the danger was gone. The resort owners even joined the small remaining group for meals and surfing. Surviving this last week had created a sort of bond among them.

Tonight, Friday, was their last dinner together, and Iris felt sad at the prospect of leaving the next morning. Five of them gathered in the pavilion around Sammy's bar, drinking their usual exotic cocktails and waiting for Kelly to join them.

"Did you see that S.J.'s podcast is trending?" Lisa passed an impressive Hemingway daiquiri over to Iris. "She made it sound like the OIJ solved the mystery all by themselves. I wonder where she gets her information. While I'm relieved S.J. didn't blow Kelly's cover, she could have credited you and Luc for all the critical discoveries you made."

Iris waved a dismissive hand. "That's quite alright. We'd rather stay under the radar." She gave Luc a sideways glance. He was smiling into his drink. Iris went on, "but I've been meaning to ask, why did you get S.J. involved if Kelly was already investigating the crime?"

Lisa gave her a sidewise glance. "This was the best tip we'd gotten in six months—that the ringleader would be here for a brief period. We couldn't afford to let him or her slip away. S.J. has quite a reputation for solving cold cases, so we thought she might provide useful intel to supplement Interpol's. I don't know why we didn't anticipate her broadcasting her suspicions about all the guests. Sorry about that."

Iris stirred her cocktail with a stick of pineapple and said nothing. She was relieved for a change of subject when Kelly entered the pavilion, visibly out of breath and still wearing a serious-looking pantsuit.

"Sorry, I didn't have time to change. I've been negotiating with Alvarez to have Margo tried first in the US, and now the Mexican authorities want a piece of her."

Sierra's expression turned curious. "What happens when there are three jurisdictions like this?"

"We negotiate," Kelly explained. "Margo was responsible for a murder in the US," she glanced over at her mother, "and one in Costa Rica. Dad was an Interpol agent, so I convinced Alvarez to extradite Margo to the US to face federal charges there first. That will, no doubt, result in a long sentence. After she's finally released from prison back home, she'll have to serve her sentences in the other two countries. She'll be locked up for the rest of her life."

Lisa gave a small shake of her head and sighed. They all stood there, eyes on the floor, in strained silence. Kelly broke the somber mood by asking Sammy to pour her several tequila shots. After a few moments, he passed her a tray with three shot glasses and accompaniments.

Cal frowned. "How can anyone commit crimes like that?"

Kelly licked salt off the back of her hand, drank a shot, then sucked on a wedge of lime. She set the rind back on the tray. "One percent of any population is composed of psychopaths. They have no moral compass and feel no remorse."

Luc tried to lighten the mood. "Do you know if they found the artifacts that Margo stole?"

Kelly brightened. "Yes, they located the entire animal quartet. Three were hidden inside big pots and stashed in a storage unit registered to Margo's art gallery. The Crying Crocodile was intercepted on its way to the gallery, allowing us to collar another member of Margo's ring. Alvarez says the artifacts will be sent back to the National Museum of Costa Rica in San José, where they'll have state-of-the-art security. Unfortunately, the Mexican pieces had already been sold on the black market. We'll keep an eye out in case they turn up at auction, but I'd expect the new owners to lie low for a while."

She went through her efficient tequila downing routine again with the next shot. "And Mom, they're going to display the quartet in its own room and call it the Pierre Duval Gallery after Dad. Someone made an anonymous donation to set that up."

At this news, Lisa bit her lip, and her eyes turned misty.

Iris noticed Sierra shoot Cal a quick smile. Sierra had mentioned earlier that requests had flooded the resort's reservation line. Apparently, everyone now wanted to take a luxury surfing vacation at "the murder resort." Iris guessed that the resort owners were behind this anonymous bequest to the National Museum.

After dinner, Iris and Luc strolled along the beach holding hands.

"I asked Cal why he'd warned us against walking on the beach at night," Luc said. "Turns out he was afraid a guest might encounter the jaguar when it was out hunting. That's why he had an armed guard patrolling this beach after dark, making sure the animal didn't make it around the resort's fence."

"I don't see a guard now."

"Cal told me that the wildlife rangers moved the jaguar further inland, away from the villages."

Iris tried not to think about what that fierce creature might have done to Mateo. They reached the stone breakwater and climbed over the rocks to the next beach.

The moon floated out from behind a cloud. "Is that a waning gibbous moon?" Iris asked.

"I believe it is smarty-pants."

"Despite everything, I'm going to miss this place. It feels like we've been here for a month."

"It's beautiful," Luc said. "It will be hard to fall asleep back in Cambridge without the sound of breaking waves."

"There's an app to provide that. I certainly won't miss wondering who in our group might be a murderer."

Luc wrapped his good arm around Iris's shoulder and pulled her close. "You know, now I think I understand how you get yourself mixed up in these dangerous situations. You don't try to stick your neck out. In fact, I was probably more reckless than you were. But when these events happen, you're good at connecting clues and helping resolve them."

Does that mean he no longer thinks I'm an adrenaline junkie?

"And I'm glad I got to see how well you're able to protect yourself. And others. I feel reassured."

They walked on, the sand sliding through their toes, the two of them swallowed by the darkness.

Iris shivered. If only she felt equally reassured.

AN INDEPENDENT AUTHOR'S REQUEST

I want to say a huge thank you for choosing to read *The Crying Crocodile*. If you enjoyed it, I would be grateful if you would write a review on the site where you purchased this book. I would love to hear what you think, and it makes such a difference helping new readers to discover my books for the first time.

To keep up to date about the next installment in the Iris Reid Mystery Series, please sign up for my newsletter: www.susancory.com You'll get a free exclusive copy of Designing Woman, interviews about Iris Reid with four of the people closest to her.

Thanks again!
Susan Cory

ACKNOWLEDGMENTS

I would like to thank the following people for their invaluable feedback: my intrepid Sisters-in-Crime writing group and my eagle-eyed beta readers: Janice Schupak and Susan Blanker. Special thanks go to my editor, Daniel Tenney for his invaluable advice and suggestions.

Authors are nothing without their readers. I can't thank you enough for reading my books, for recommending them, and for writing reviews.

www.ingramcontent.com/pod-product-compliance
Lightning Source LLC
LaVergne TN
LVHW010158070526
838199LV00062B/4409